RAILROAD TO PERDITION

ALSO BY MARK GREATHOUSE

The Frontier Chronicles

Perilous Trails

Wyoming Calls

Longhorns North

Warpath

Hunter Vs. Hunted

Freedom Drovers

A Poison Spreads

Darkness Looms

The Tumbleweed Sagas

Nueces Justice

Nueces Reprise

Nueces Deceit

Nueces Blood

Nueces Grit

Nueces Truth

Nueces Legend

The Tumbleweed Sagas: Junior's Story

Lone Star Vigilante: Justice Texas Style

Guns on the Guadalupe: Justice on the River

RAILROAD TO PERDITION

JUSTICE RIDES AN IRON HORSE

THE TUMBLEWEED SAGAS
BOOK 10

MARK GREATHOUSE

WOLFPACK
PUBLISHING
— EST 2013 —

Railroad to Perdition: Justice Rides an Iron Horse
Paperback Edition
Copyright © 2025 by Mark Greathouse

Wolfpack Publishing
1707 E. Diana Street
Tampa, Florida 33610

www.wolfpackpublishing.com

Paperback ISBN 979-8-89567-739-1
Ebook ISBN 979-8-89567-738-4
LCCN 2025947410

Dedicated with love to my wife, Carolyn, and to our two sons, Mike and Matt.

MAP OF TEXAS

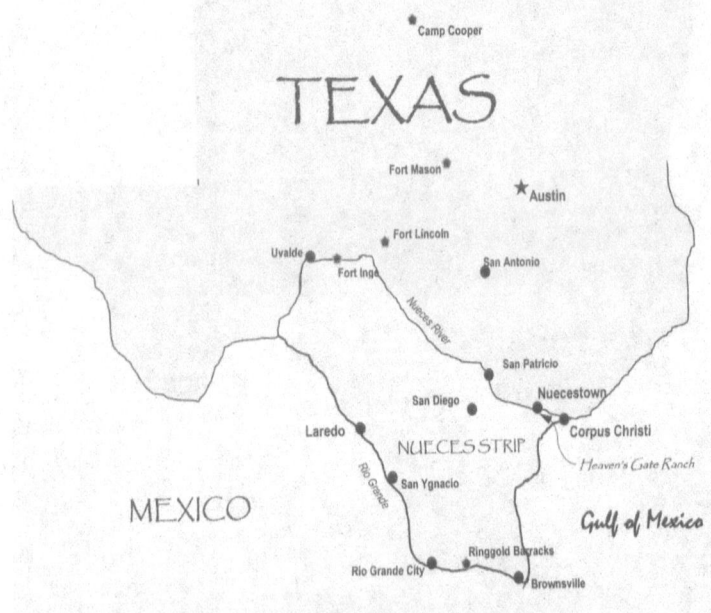

The vast Nueces Strip serves as the primary setting for the
Tumbleweed Sagas. The Strip was also called Wild Horse Desert,
owing to the millions of Mustangs that roamed its prairies. *(Sketch
by Mark Greathouse)*

NUECESTOWN

Nuecestown, Texas, established in 1852 by English and German settlers, was developed by Corpus Christi founder Colonel Henry Kinney along the Nueces River as a ferry crossing. Mostly thanks to the railroad passing it by, it's now a "ghost town" marked only by historical markers. All that remains is a preserved schoolhouse and the old Nuecestown Cemetery. By 1896, the town was struggling economically due to the railroads passing it by. *(Sketch by Mark Greathouse)*

THE CAST

Lucas Dunn, Jr.—*Goes by the nickname "Junior." The proverbial fruit doesn't grow far from the tree, as Junior follows in the lawman footsteps of his legendary Texas Ranger father.*

Cassie McCully Dunn—*Daughter of Grant McCully, who owned a ranch near Heaven's Gate Ranch. Cassie is married to Junior. Children are Shawn and Bode.*

Grant McCully—*Cassie's father. McCully is a successful rancher.*

Lucas "Long Luke" Dunn—*Was one of the greatest Texas Ranger Captains ever, having gained repute as Indian fighter and respected lawman. Comanche called him Ghost-Who-Rides. Luke builds Heaven's Gate Ranch and has eleven children with his wife Elisa.*

Elisa Corrigan Dunn—*Married Luke Dunn after losing her family to frontier rigors, including fighting off Comanche and hired killers.*

Garth Jones—*A gunfighter for hire.*

Arturo Garcia—*Deputy US Marshal assigned to central Texas.*

King Callahan—*Power-hungry owner of a large South Texas ranch.*

Irma Callahan—*King Callahan's temptress wife.*

Brody & Tess—*Junior's Blue Lacy dogs.*

Buffalo Watts—*Famed mountain man who lived long enough to retire to Corpus Christi after a life of trapping, buffalo hunting, and stalking Indians for the Army.*

Kyle McClintock—*Friend to Junior Dunn.*

Landry Giles—*Financial executive with the Southern Pacific Railroad.*

Carolina Giles—*California socialite and daughter to Landry Giles.*

Gordon Murphy—*Financier from New York City with interests in oil and railroads.*

HISTORICAL CHARACTERS

Charles Culberson—*Followed Jim Hogg and then Joseph Clay Stiles Blackburn as governor of Texas. He ran afoul of the Democratic Party over his opposition to the Ku Klux Klan.*
John Reynolds Hughes—*Became the longest-serving Texas Ranger captain. Hughes dealt with Comanche and Apache over his years as a rancher and lawman. He was a sergeant in the Frontier Battalion down along the Texas/Mexico border until 1893, when he was promoted to captain.*
Emilio Forto—*Sheriff of Cameron County, TX, and later mayor of Brownsville.*
Archer Parr—*Known as "Archie," he established a political dynasty in what became Jim Wells County and led to decades of Democratic Party control through means fair and foul.*
Stephen Powers—*Political power broker exercising tight control over goings on in Corpus Christi. He has close ties with Archie Parr and Jim Wells.*
John William Vann—*Tax Collector and Sheriff of Kerr County, TX from 1892 through 1902.*
Judge Isaac Parker—*Known as the "hanging judge," Parker*

delivered law and order out of Fort Smith, Arkansas. Bass Reeves reported to him.

John McTiernan—*Sheriff of Nueces County, TX from 1896 to 1902.*

Henry Thomas—*Sheriff of Galveston, Texas.*

Uriah Lott—*Railroad entrepreneur who founded several railroads in Texas.*

James O. Taylor—*Sheriff of Bee County, Texas.*

John H. Reagan—*First chairman of the Railroad Commission of Texas.*

William G. Crush—*Staged a crash of locomotives as a publicity stunt in 1896.*

Robert Kleberg—*Married Alice Gertrudis King and became the owner of the huge King Ranch.*

W.T. "Brack" Morris—*Sheriff of Karnes County, Texas.*

John Hillard Dunn—*Railroad entrepreneur and lifelong railroad man.*

John "Red John" Dunn—*Retired Texas Ranger who rode with Captains Wallace and McNelly.*

THEME

Justice:
The quality of being just, impartial, or fair per the principle or ideal of just dealing or proper action in conformance to a principle or ideal as defined by the law or to truth, fact, or reason.

YOU'RE INVITED

Howdy,

You can call me Junior. In fact, this can be called Tumbleweed Sagas: Junior's Story. I'm right pleased to have taken up where the story of my legendary dad left off, as he brought lawbreakers to justice as a Texas Ranger. I expect it runs strong in my ancestral blood.

Railroad to Perdition: Justice Rides an Iron Horse picks up my story from *Guns on the Guadalupe: Justice on the River*. Like the prequels, it offers a twisted tale of intrigue, as I must solve the mystery of a series of robberies, graft, and connected killings during the construction of a South Texas railroad. The Nueces Strip, encompassing the southern tip of Texas by this time, could be said to be afire economically, as agriculture, railroads, communications, and black gold spawned ever greater growth. Communications? While the telegraph expanded its reach, it was the soon-to-be-ubiquitous telephone that was beginning to make its presence felt mostly in the larger Texas cities. And black gold? The "Lucas Gusher" at Spindletop Hill in 1901 near Beaumont would eventually usher in the Texas oil era. Gushers of oil would become ever more common, sending geysers of money into bank accounts.

Barbed wire had made its appearance on the Nueces Strip fifteen years earlier and was creating a topographical patchwork of pasture and farm. The resulting range wars, fence cuttings, and water rights battles fostered lawbreaking challenges that tested the mettle of many a lawman. Lynching and worse bore evidence to a rise in vigilante justice, as frustrated and fearful citizens took the law into their own hands.

It's 1897, and the Nueces Strip could be inhospitable six ways to Sunday. Mottes or small clusters of live oak or mesquite offered occasional shade relief on the sunbaked prairies. The often-dry creek beds and arroyos eventually filled with rainwater and emptied into Nueces Bay and... farther to the east...Corpus Christi Bay. Flash flooding was an ongoing fear. Summers? Well, they tended to be hot and humid. Weather was pretty much whatever you wanted, if you waited long enough.

The abundant animal life on the Nueces Strip featured deer, javelina, fox, coyote, lynx, black bear, and mountain lion. Armadillos and prairie dogs competed for prairie real estate. At one point, horses were more numerous on the Strip than any animal, including humans. Occasionally, spotted ocelots and even wolves could be sighted by the practiced eye. Owls, hawks, eagles, buzzards...they abounded. Come spring, wildflowers swept across much of the landscape, painted like a huge rainbow, with scarlet sage, hibiscus, daisies, poppies, lilies, and the ubiquitous bluebonnets. Groves of cypress, juniper, and palmetto could be found. Pecan trees drew their sustenance from rich soil along the Nueces River. The very name *"nueces"* was Spanish for nuts. Cactus, along with yucca and agave, abounded. The Nueces Strip surely served as God's canvas.

If you were on foot, it was advisable to keep an eye and ear peeled for rattlesnakes. They tended to blend in fairly well with their surroundings, so their rattle was often folks' first and only warning of an impending attack. The rattlesnake spawned many a "Texas-ism" like "he's so bad he has rattlesnake fangs and twice the venom" or "he's so tough, he cuddles with rattlesnakes."

The similarities between natural and human dangers were often striking. Imagine the intense yellow eyes and tense muscles of a mountain lion on the hunt. A doe looks about innocently unaware. The lion's tail twitches ever-so-slightly. Patience...of sorts. The moment of attack must be exactly right. Only that infinitesimal twitch of the tip of his tail reveals the tension as he is about to launch himself. He dares not indulge even a blink of his eyes. The doe sniffs the air and dips her head to feed. The mountain lion's muscled haunches spring him forward with claws splayed. His jaws grasp the doe's neck in a death grip. In its vast silence, the Nueces Strip sucks it all in. Danger was a constant.

Application of the law could too often be horrifically fast or mind-bogglingly slow. The accused lawbreaker could as easily meet his end at an impromptu necktie party as be convicted in a court of law. Fingerprint matching and DNA databases were nonexistent. My own cousin Red John Dunn capped off a ten-year enlistment with the Texas Rangers under Captain Bland Chamberlain and later Captain Leander McNelly with several instances of involvement with vigilante justice. Taking the law into one's own hands was expeditious but illegal and fraught with far too many instances of innocent men being on the wrong end of a rope or bullet. Dunn himself was tried twice for murder and acquitted both times.

With *Railroad to Perdition: Justice Rides an Iron Horse*, I'm right pleased to share my story of building upon my legendary father's lawman footsteps and seeking to make significant headway in bringing justice to Texas. Blood, as shed by both innocent and evil men, colors the Strip. Desperate killers, rustlers, disease, and savages are part and parcel to my life. Just about anywhere I ride, death could be reaching for my reins. While it could be said that I emulate my father in building considerable notoriety and creating enemies by virtue of my success in bringing lawbreakers to justice, I am very much my own man and have begun to establish reliable allies.

While the "Cast of Historical Characters" provides some helpful true-to-life framework to the life and times in Texas, woven into *Railroad to Perdition: Justice Rides an Iron Horse* are actual settlers as drawn from my own Irish ancestors committed to taming the frontier. Such real-life characters, coupled with actual events, have served to reinforce the fictional setting with a strong dose of historical reality.

For anyone of a mind that the frontier had been won, they had a second think coming. The wild prairies and hills of Texas were alive and kicking, lawbreaking was very much in abundance, and what one might call the residuals of old wild west justice prevailed. It's in this setting that the need for justice remained strong for better or worse.

Kindly,
Lucas Dunn, Jr.

RAILROAD TO PERDITION

PROLOGUE

I TOOK my time rubbing down and talking to Tornado before returning to the big house. The big Appaloosa stallion deserved every stroke of the curry brush. It gave me time to think. I found myself swelling with pride just a bit, as I thought back on the past few months. I'd solved a mystery that had baffled the best lawmen around these parts by bringing to justice a cunning vigilante. Skill? Some. Luck? Some of that, too. My father, a legendary Texas Ranger, was quite justly bust-a-button proud. Then, I'd solved a series of murders on the Guadalupe River as part of a land grab scheme.

Garth Jones slipped from the saddle of his heavily-breathing, well-lathered horse. He released reins slick with his blood. Looking at the mangled mess that was his right hand, he cursed the Texas Ranger. He'd underestimated his foe and paid a dear price. He tightened the tourniquet around his wrist. The pain was excruciating. The fugitive looked back from whence he'd come. "I won't forget you, Lucas Dunn," he hissed.

Jones took a swig of water and remounted. He needed a doctor, but had to escape these parts before a posse could be mustered. There'd be plenty of time for revenge.

The note that Johnnie Crockett had delivered weighed heavily on my thoughts. I knew it was from Garth Jones despite it having been unsigned. It'd been six months since the shooting, but he hadn't forgotten. That was no surprise considering how my bullet had mangled his hand. Jones held a serious grudge.

Watch your back, Ranger. Yep. It haunted me.

I finished up with Tornado and washed my hands and face as best I could in the washbasin.

Cassie greeted me at the door with baby Sean in her arms. "Did you hear from Captain Hughes?" She laid our young son in a cradle by the kitchen table.

"Yep," I responded with a nod and a smile.

"And?" Cassie absentmindedly fingered the Texas Ranger badge pinned to my chest as though continually accommodating the life of a lawman's wife. "Is he dead?" She had to ask.

Regret surged through me as I shook my head. "I expect he's still around. His grudge against me likely keeps him alive." Hatred was a hell of a motivator for evil folks. The Texas Ranger in me wondered whether Captain Hughes would let me track Jones down or leave it to someone with no personal connection.

ONE
I MEET AN IRON HORSE

HOW HOT WAS IT? The sweat running off the backs of the laborers could have refilled the buckets about as fast as the men could drink the lukewarm brownish water from the Nueces River. It hadn't been that long ago that folks in nearby Corpus Christi had relied on great barrels of water brought by mostly Mexican merchants when they weren't relying on great cisterns or artesian wells. The city was finally served by a public water system beginning in 1893. Water? That didn't diminish the effect of hundred-degree temperatures and high humidity.

Evenings brought only a modicum of relief.

There were more than ten thousand miles of railroad crisscrossing Texas, and most of it had been constructed under brutal weather and environment conditions. Crews were comprised of a mix of races, so it was unsurprising that prejudices drove emotions still held from four decades ago in the wake of the War Between the States. While liquor wasn't approved, it was tolerated in the work camps. Booze tended to bring passions to the surface, and fights among laborers often erupted. Supervisors mostly let the disruptions run their course so long as lives weren't at risk.

I heard from a cousin of an incident where a group of Blacks gathered in a vigilante-style confrontation with a supervisor to demand better conditions comparable to what they felt White laborers were receiving. The sun had just set and the men were heavily liquored up.

A sweaty, blustering, barrel-chested foreman led the way to the supervisor's tent. "Mistuh Trent! Mistuh Trent!" he called out. "Come out, Mistuh Trent!" The atmosphere was electric with tension.

Trent emerged from his tent clothed in red long-john underwear, a broad-brimmed hat, and boots. He held a 10-gauge shotgun in the crook of his arm. "What y'all be wanting this time of night?" he drawled.

"Dem Whities gittin' mo watuh than us!" growled the foreman.

"Yer full of crap, Dixon. Y'all go back to yer tents," directed Trent.

"Water...water...water," began the chant echoed among the twenty laborers backing Dixon.

Trent had been through this before. He fully appreciated what drove these and others to complain of their plights. It was rough work. He didn't much like the water either, but there was a railroad to build. The men didn't seem inclined to disperse easily. "What y'all want, Dixon?" he finally asked.

Dixon looked at the 10-gauge shotgun. "We needs a break, Mistuh Trent," he finally got to the truth of the matter. "We be workin' harder than them Whities."

Dixon nodded. His peripheral vision caught movement to his right. An angry, drunken gang of White and Mexican laborers was approaching with clubs and hammers in hand.

The air reeked of sweat and liquor. As they charged, an explosion shattered the air. A crater appeared between the two groups. Everyone froze. Trent calmly inserted a fresh shell in the shotgun. There was silence but for the click as Trent pulled back the hammer. "Go to your tents," he said firmly.

Amid grumbling and drunken stumbling, the men dispersed. Trent shook his head.

✯✯

Tornado reared. It was unlike him, but I had to admit that the blast of steam and squealing of steel on steel was unnerving.

Setting there before me was the San Antonio & Aransas Pass Railroad's very first steam locomotive, a Baldwin. It had been built about a decade ago at the Baldwin Locomotive Works back east in Philadelphia, Pennsylvania.

Tornado surely was asking what we were doing here at the Corpus Christi railyard of the SA&AP Railroad. As Captain Hughes had informed me, a transportation entrepreneur named Uriah Lott was intent on building railroads all over South Texas. Lott's SA&AP Railroad was developed to connect San Antonio with Aransas Bay on Texas' Gulf coast, where a deepwater port was being developed. There had been a problem with railroad work crews, mostly along racial and cultural lines.

Most of the work was the repair of existing track and addition of sidings, as Lott's enterprise had been forced into receivership a few years back. In 1892, the line was acquired by the Southern Pacific Railroad, though the SP failed to integrate the SA&AP into its system. The acquisition overlooked the SP's new control of a *parallel and competing line* in violation of the Texas Constitution at the time, and this would eventually foment serious problems from competitors.

There was more. Two teamsters, the crews that delivered rails, ties, nails, and the like to the line crews, had been killed. Lott didn't believe that the killings were accidental.

There I sat, surveying the scene before me. Work crews sweated profusely under a broiling South Texas sun. Folks described it as so hot that chickens were laying hard-boiled eggs. The weather was tough on man and beast. Add back-breaking labor and the dangers of dehydration, let alone bone-crushing hammer blows on steel nails, and I figured these men were on a mental knife's edge.

They were a diverse lot of multiple races and cultural backgrounds. Demon whiskey could loosen the fetters of civil restraint enough to let fly raw emotions from the residue of deeply embedded historical conflicts. Might that drive some to murder? It sure seemed like there was plenty of fuel. Add oxygen and heat to the mix, and the result is fire. Laborers were protective of their own. That is to say, there weren't loose tongues flapping with facts or rumors about the demise of the two teamsters. Even when loosened with booze, they tended to be a tight-lipped lot.

I hadn't gone into this totally blind. My cousin John Hillard Dunn was but a teen but was fixing to put a teamster business together to serve Uriah Lott's proposed St. Louis, Brownsville, & Mexico Railroad that would cut past Corpus Christi and connect with the southernmost tip of Texas. We chatted about teamster crews over beers in Nuecestown.

"Anything special I should know, cousin?"

Dunn leaned forward as though to impart some great wisdom. "They can be an unruly bunch, not unlike the line crews. They have incentives."

I nodded expectantly.

"They get paid for the quantity of rails, ties, and the like that they deliver each day. The more delivered, the more money they make. Anything that gets in their way can stir up serious delivery problems. These deaths you mentioned? Well, they represent just such a problem. The teamsters are averse to being shot at, much less killed."

Dunn shared the nature of the teams, wagons, and drivers. Like the line crews, they were a diverse lot and strong as oxen, given the cargo they had to handle and the rough landscape they were required to cover.

I was grateful to my cousin and thought on his advice as I scanned the scene before me. I checked the loads in my Winchester carbine and Smith & Wesson revolver. One could never be too careful where volatile situations might be faced.

With Corpus Christi and my introduction to the SA&AP behind me, I rode into Skidmore a tad south of Beeville. Construction of a siding was underway under that ever-present broiling Texas sun.

I rode up to what was labeled as the foreman's tent and dismounted. "Mr. Jenkins?" I asked upon peering into the tent with its flaps pulled back to permit what little breeze there was to flow through.

A portly gentleman with rolled-up shirtsleeves and a sweat-stained straw hat and shirt looked up from his desk and laid a squinty-eyed look on me. "That's me. Who you be?"

"Texas Ranger Lucas Dunn, Junior, Mr. Jenkins. Captain Hughes sent me to look into a problem y'all have been having concerning crew violence. I expect the folks at the Southern Pacific requested our help."

Jenkins offered a wry smile, leaned back in his chair, and began fanning himself. "About damned time," he flatly stated. "Teamsters are so damned scared, they're requesting armed guards."

I nodded.

"You know anything about the railroad construction business, Ranger Dunn?" he asked, likely as a challenge to ease his mind some as to my ability to deal with his problem.

"Enough, Mr. Jenkins," I responded. I didn't reckon to go into detail, as he surely knew plenty more than me. I surely didn't want to open my mouth and show him what little I knew.

"Hrumph!" groused Jenkins. "They only sent one of you?"

With that, I couldn't help but smile. "As folks say, Mr. Jenkins, one fight, one Ranger."

"You seem right young, Ranger Dunn. You solved these sorts of cases before?" he asked quite naturally.

"Captain Hughes assigned this case to me because I have." It was the honest, unvarnished truth.

"What do you propose to do?" asked Jenkins.

"First, I'd like to hear what you know of the situation. Then, I figure to check with the sheriff. After that, I'll chat with some of the line crew and teamsters you recommend. Once that's done? Well, let's see where all of that leads." I scratched my chin tentatively.

"Are you by chance...?"

"Luke Dunn's son. Yes." Would I ever escape the comparison with my legendary father?

★★

Jenkins filled me in on the particulars, as he understood them. Now, I reckoned to hear what Sheriff James Taylor could add.

I must say that I was impressed with the Bee County jail. It was a Victorian-style, two-story structure with a mansard roof. It was imposing to say the least, and I figure no lawbreaker in his right mind would care to take residence.

The massive entry door creaked loudly as I pushed it open. The thing could surely have awakened the dead.

"Who goes?" came a challenging voice from behind a large desk in the dimly lit foyer. A pair of eyes stared up from under the brim of a white cowboy-creased hat. He looked to be a deputy.

I blinked a couple of times in a vain attempt to quickly adjust my eyes to the shadows. "Texas Ranger Lucas Dunn here to see Sheriff Taylor," I replied as confidently as I could muster.

"Business?" the deputy asked.

"SA&AP killings. Captain Hughes sent me."

"Humph. Sheriff be upstairs. Hang tight, and I'll go fetch him."

I stood unmoving and waited patiently while the deputy made his way up a flight of stairs. He must have been around a while, as I saw gray hair peeking from under his hat. He walked slowly and with a decided limp and slightly slumped shoulders.

Taylor came clomping down the stairs. A big man, his weight made a solid impression on the stairs. "Welcome, Ranger Dunn," he greeted as he reached the bottom step. We shook hands, and he invited me into his office. As we entered, I saw the deputy safely negotiate the last stair and find his way to the security of his desk.

"Pleased to meet you, Sheriff," I said upon taking a seat opposite the sheriff's desk.

Taylor offered me a cigar.

"Thanks, but I generally don't smoke or drink."

Taylor laughed. "I didn't until I took this job." He clipped the end of the cigar, lit up, and took a few pulls. A single column of cigar smoke spiraled upward. "Deputy says you're here about the SA&AP matter."

I nodded.

"Have you talked with Jenkins?"

I nodded again.

Taylor blew a smoke ring and leaned back in his chair. "Railroading is damned competitive, Ranger."

"Seems competitive enough to do some killing," I observed.

"To be straight, my jail is full up. I haven't had time to mess with the railroad killings."

"What can you tell me that Jenkins might have missed?" I asked.

Another smoke ring went up. "The killings were done two days apart. Both victims were shot in the torso with a close-range follow-up kill shot to the head. The shootings were in broad daylight within two hundred yards of the rail spur. No one claimed to witness the killings. The killer wore black and used a rifle and a revolver. Slugs were both .38 caliber. Plenty of them around of course. Oh, and there was a third attempt, but the shooter missed. Sure wore thin on the work crew."

The killings were obviously done by a paid professional gunman. "Other than the kill-shots, you've corroborated what Jenkins told me. Any thoughts on who might be behind this?"

Taylor smiled. "Uriah Lott has a few enemies. He had

some financial troubles a few years back. That's why the Southern Pacific bought the SA&AP. As to motive, there are folks east of here concerned with rumors of Lott wanting to build a line from St. Louis to Mexico."

"You think Archer Parr might be playing in this game?" I asked.

"Is there a game that Parr isn't playing in?" Taylor replied rhetorically.

"From what I know of Parr, he wouldn't risk his political career with murder," I observed.

Taylor tapped his head as though recalling something he'd forgotten to mention. "I did hear that one of the rail crew said that the killer held the revolver in his left hand and carried the rifle in the crook of his right elbow."

"Well, I appreciate your time, Sheriff. I'll do a bit of digging on my own."

"If I learn more, I'll let you know, Ranger."

"Where can a hungry lawman get a good meal around here, Sheriff?"

"Head over to Martha Embry's place up the street. Good grub at fair prices."

I stood, shook Taylor's hand, and exited the jail. The deputy was huddled behind a stack of wanted posters.

Skidmore seemed a welcoming place loaded with typical Texas hospitality. Martha's place was near the train station. By now, Tornado was becoming accustomed to the locomotive. He was still a tad wild-eyed but stood stock still as I hitched the reins to the iron post. The restaurant looked friendly enough. A bell jingled as I entered. The aroma of fresh-brewed coffee wafted in the air.

"Just grab any seat," came a female voice from behind the door to the kitchen. "Be with you in a minute."

I eased over to a nearby table.

"Help yourself to coffee," added the voice, friendly-like, as I was about to sit.

I didn't have to be asked twice. Grabbing what looked to be a clean ceramic cup, I filled it with the steaming-hot brew. It smelled right good. I returned to the table and sat.

A comely-looking middle-aged woman with hair pulled back in a bun approached. "My name's Martha. What will you be having, cowboy?" Her eyes shifted, focusing in on my badge. "I mean, Texas Ranger."

"Been called both, ma'am," I said with a smile. "Own a spread down toward Corpus."

She nodded. "Got bacon today. Goes great with eggs and biscuits."

"Sounds great, thanks."

She was about to turn away but paused. "You here about them murders?"

"You know something special?" I asked.

"I think the man who done them ate breakfast here." She gave me a concerned look. "Sort of swarthy-looking fellow. Wore black. Wore his gun on his left hip." She scratched her head. "His right hand was mangled a bit. Nasty looking."

I nearly spat out a mouthful of coffee, but managed to swallow. Her description of the killer matched what I'd heard from Jenkins and Taylor, but that last sentence caught my full attention. She'd just described my old nemesis, Garth Jones. In a gun battle at Heaven's Gate Ranch, one of my bullets had hit his hand as it held the receiver of his rifle. Evil soul that he was, Jones would surely love to pay me back for crippling him. I gathered my wits as best I could. "I'm grateful for you telling me."

"I'll get them eggs an' fixings." She smiled and scurried off to the kitchen.

As I waited, I found myself looking forward to interviewing railroad crew members. Even if it was in fact Garth Jones, I knew he didn't work for free. Someone was behind the killings. Lassoing Jones wouldn't solve the case.

TWO
QUESTIONS

I VISITED BRIEFLY with Jenkins to be sure he had no problem with me questioning his crews. I admit to being unusually excited owing to Martha's description of what she reckoned to be the killer.

"It's hotter than Hades, Ranger. Shade is scarce out here. You're welcome to use my tent. I'll mosey up the line." Jenkins had a folding fan that he was making good use of.

"Thanks, Mr. Jenkins. If you could have your men visit me one at a time, that would be helpful. I'll try not to keep them long from their labors."

One by one, crew members left their work to see me. A few moments in the shade were likely a welcome relief. The first couple of interviews were short. Two Black men claimed not to have seen anything. The third crewman theorized that one of the Blacks must have done the killings. I was beginning to think that this was going to be a nonproductive exercise.

It sure enough was hot. Little wonder that folks down this neck of the prairies enjoyed hot peppers, as they made the air seem cooler by comparison. I picked up the fan

Jenkins had left behind and put it to good use. A sweaty Mexican tracklayer sauntered into the tent.

"*Habla Inglés?*" I asked.

"Damn right, Mr. Texas Ranger," he informed me with a nearly toothless smile. He was obviously proud of his mastery of English.

"I'm Texas Ranger Dunn. You know what I'm here for?"

"Yes. My name is Arturo Garcia. You want to know what I saw of the killings." He wrung the sweat from the floppy hat he held.

"And?" I asked.

"Saw it clear as day. Slender White man dressed in black. Maybe a hundred yards off. Got one, came back a couple of days later and got the second. Fired one shots each time. Got both teamsters dead center in their chests. Damned accurate sonofabitch. Rode off on a black horse." The Mexican smiled. "That's what I saw, Mr. Texas Ranger." Garcia paused. "He tried a third day but missed." He chuckled. "Guess he had a bad day."

"Did he fire the rifle left-handed or right-handed?" I followed up.

The Mexican scratched his chin thoughtfully. "Left-handed. I think his right hand was not good. Yes. He rested the forestock on his right forearm."

I nodded appreciatively. I was getting the impression that this tracklayer was working below his ability level. "What did you do before laying rails?"

He shrugged. "Why you ask?"

"Just curious," I replied.

Garcia gazed at me, trying to figure out whether he could trust me. "I spent three years at Huntsville for a robbery I didn't do. Before that, I studied law at the University of Texas. Grew up on a ranch near Brownsville."

I reckoned there was plenty more to the story, but I had

more interviews ahead. "I'd like to know more, Mr. Garcia. Care to meet for some *cerveza* later?"

"I don't drink."

"Meet me at Martha's. I'll buy you dinner." I had a feeling that a good man lurked beneath the exterior of this man. It looked to me as though he'd tangled with somebody with enough influence to stick him in jail.

Garcia nodded and headed back to his crew.

I interviewed eight more crew members and two teamsters, gaining little or no new information. As I laid the fan on the rickety old desk and stood, Jenkins returned.

"Learn anything new?" he asked.

"Nothing to stir a rattlesnake," I responded with a slight head shake.

"Not surprised. They're a tight-lipped bunch." Jenkins was drenched in sweat. He wrung out his bandana and picked up the fan.

"What's the story with that Garcia fellow?" I had to ask.

Jenkins gave me a curious look. "Hard worker. Got a burr in his saddle over something. Damned greaser. He a problem for you?"

It was clear that Jenkins never bothered to find out what that burr was. It was also clear that he held Mexicans in contempt; not uncommon in Texas. "He told me what I needed to know." I wrung out my own bandana. "I have some folks to talk with. If I need more, I'll look you up, Mr. Jenkins." I shook his damp hand and departed.

Plenty of questions lingered in my mind as I mounted Tornado. A few words with Archer Parr about the railroad business in Texas seemed to be in order. Heavy on my mind was that Garth Jones was prowling the area. I would eventually have to deal with the hired gun. A showdown of any kind wouldn't do, as I needed to find out whose payroll he was on. Killing him wouldn't get me any answers. Somebody had it in for Uriah Lott in a big way, and I aimed to find out who that was. Meanwhile, I'd have a rendezvous at Martha's restaurant in a couple of hours.

I headed to the place where the killings had taken place. While I lamented the lack of a fresh crime scene, I reckoned to gather whatever evidence might still linger. I rode along about a mile of completed track to the place marked out neatly with tiny flags by Sheriff Taylor. I scanned the area. The only cover was a stand of mesquite about a hundred yards south of the tracks. Jones, if in fact he was the shooter, would have had the sun behind him. I walked Tornado to the spot that seemed optimum to me. Five minutes of looking around yielded two .30-40 casings glistening in the afternoon sun. How on earth had the sheriff missed them? The casings were another possible confirmation of Garth Jones' handiwork, assuming he'd acquired another Winchester like the one I'd destroyed. The old habits of hired guns were pretty much unchanging.

As I strode into her restaurant, Martha nodded to the coffee pot. For whatever reason, she didn't offer coffee service to her customers. Of the eight tables, all but two were occupied. The customers appeared to be locals, far as I could tell. There were two couples, a family of four, and three tables occupied by an eclectic collection of men. Two were obviously cowhands, and another with a bowler hung on a post beside the table looked to be a banker or attorney. I received a couple of nods upon sightings of my Texas Ranger badge, as I carried my coffee to an empty table.

"You don't want to sit there, Mr. Ranger," advised Martha. "That's King Callahan's table." She motioned to the other empty table setting against the far wall.

Naturally, she left me wondering who this King Callahan might be. My inclination was to take the seat anyway, but I wasn't here to make trouble. I grabbed a seat at the far table. As I sipped my coffee, I took the time to scan the room and observe the guests. A few were immersed in animated conversations. The bowler man quietly picked at his dinner. He seemed none too happy.

"Tonight's special is roast buffalo steak wrapped in bacon. Otherwise, it's meatloaf and taters or spaghetti," came Martha's voice as though appearing from nowhere. "What will it be?"

"I'm waiting for a guest. Give me a few minutes, Martha," I responded. Just as I finished speaking, I felt the hush fall over the room like a frozen blanket.

Arturo Garcia strode into the room. He wasn't the shirt-less, sweating man I'd interviewed earlier in the day. Nope. This man was well-groomed. Garcia wore a clean shirt and jeans with polished boots. A Colt Peacemaker revolver sat in a holster on his hip, and a fine cowboy-creased hat sat atop his head. He spotted me and made a beeline for the table.

I pointed to the coffee pot, but he ignored my signal. The room remained quiet enough that you could have heard a church mouse breathing.

Martha had reddened in her face a tad and looked as though she wanted to say something.

Now, it struck me that there were no Mexicans in the restaurant. I had obviously breached protocol by inviting Garcia. I stood and shook Garcia's hand. "Grab a seat, Arturo. I figured to wait for you before I ordered."

Martha eased over to our table. She was clearly uncomfortable, as the clientele were laying looks of considerable annoyance at her. Somehow deep within her soul, she mustered the strength to confront me. "Mr. Texas Ranger, we don't serve them kind." She nodded toward Garcia.

I must admit that my smile was a bit patronizing. "Well, it seems you've just had a change in that policy, Martha. I'm proud that you are able to stand up for folks regardless of race or creed."

With that, Martha flustered. A couple of diners threw money on their tables, grumbled, and left the restaurant. "You're costing me customers!" she declared.

"We'll take that special you mentioned. I like mine on the rare side."

Garcia nodded.

"His too," I stated firmly.

Martha's shoulders dropped resignedly. She couldn't muster the sand to refuse service, but was none too happy. She looked around before returning to the kitchen. She sighed. Three tables had been vacated.

Garcia smiled. He reached into his pocket and covertly drew out a Deputy US Marshal badge. He flashed it at me and stuffed it back into the pocket. No wonder he'd been so observant of the killing of the teamsters. Lawmen tend to be that way.

I chuckled. "What are you doing hammering railroad spikes?"

"That's nothing compared to sitting in a cell at Huntsville," he replied.

"Three years?" I asked.

Garcia laughed. "More like three weeks," he replied in a low voice. "I had to establish my cover. Word gets out right fast to the right folks if you've done any time at Huntsville."

"How did you wind up with the SA&AP?" I asked.

"Well, Ranger Dunn, as you might imagine, the railroad business is fraught with powerful folks doing whatever it takes to gain and hold power. Look at the Southern Pacific, for example. They bought out Lott's interest and never set foot on the SA&AP. They seized the opportunity to control another rail line. Governor Culberson's not too happy with the Railroad Commission of Texas."

Garcia was grabbing my interest. "And you're?" I pried.

"Working my way into the SP organization from the bottom up. It was simply a coincidence that I was there when those shootings happened." Garcia shook his head ruefully. "It nearly blew my cover. I got really worried when you showed up."

"Not to worry. I reckon to stay clear of your game. Any idea who's behind the killings?" I asked as Martha placed our dinners before us.

Garcia smiled and struggled to cut himself a generous slice of bison steak. "Can't say...yet."

I understood his reticence, though it was inconvenient. Garcia was answering to folks back east who hadn't a clue as to what life truly was like out here. They only knew police, courts, and judges. Bushwhackings weren't on their agenda. Their expertise lay in the power and influence surrounding politics. As to the killings, this was less about legal turf for me and more about who was paying Garth Jones. "From witness accounts, I've figured the killer to be a fellow named Garth Jones. He and I tangled a while back, and he was none too pleased with the outcome."

"Can't say that I ever heard of him. Bad one, I gather," said Garcia. He struggled to slice a piece of his bison. "Damn, but bison can be tough," he observed and put his knife aside. "And it sure isn't rare."

I cut into my own perfectly cooked steak. "Martha!" I called.

She appeared with a guilty expression written across her face.

"Fix my friend here a proper steak."

She blushed, sighed sheepishly, and carried Garcia's plate back to the kitchen.

"That was no bison steak, Arturo. Looked more like boot leather."

Garcia smiled. "I think we'll get along just fine, Lucas."

"You can call me Junior. Most folks do." I politely waited until Martha placed a properly cooked bison steak before Garcia. "You heard of that Black marshal up Oklahoma way? The one out of Fort Smith?"

"Bass Reeves?" he responded.

"Yeah. I met him last year. He gave me some advice on a series of murders. It was complicated, and I was having a tough time figuring the case out. He advised that patience was critically important, that we handled marathons, not sprints."

Martha appeared with a properly cooked bison steak. Given that it was cooked rare, we hadn't had to wait long.

"Never met Reeves, but a lot of us learned from tales we've heard about him. The son of a gun is illiterate, but it doesn't stop him. Smart as can be and tough. Collars a lot of lawbreakers." Garcia was now quite obviously enjoying his bison steak. "By the way, thanks for dealing with Martha. Hard to believe there's still folks around with those sorts of feelings."

We were giving serious thought to ordering slices of apple pie when the back door opened and a tall, well-dressed man strode in as though he owned the place. I rightly reckoned that this was King Callahan, as he went straight to the table Martha had advised me against sitting at.

The other diners gave him deferential nods as though kneeling to their master.

Callahan laid a dark look on Garcia.

Martha scurried over and even poured his coffee. "The usual, Mr. Callahan," she said.

"You know I don't like greasers in here, Martha," he snarled. "What you doing letting him in?"

We couldn't help but overhear. I nodded to Garcia, stood, and strolled over to Callahan's table. "Howdy. I'm Texas Ranger Lucas Dunn. You must be the King Callahan I've been hearing about. Pleased to make your acquaintance." I held out my hand, friendly-like.

Callahan's mouth gaped. I'd taken him completely by surprise. As if by reflex, he stood and shook my proffered hand. He remained speechless as he resumed his seat.

I caught Martha's eye. "Martha, we'll have some of that delicious apple pie you have on the counter. And do give Mr. Callahan here a slice. Our compliments." I sat down, and it was all I could do to contain a triumphant smile.

Slices of apple pie magically appeared before us, and I wasted no time taking a bite. "My compliments, Martha. This pie is downright delicious."

I saw Callahan in my peripheral vision. He still hadn't quite recovered from my bold greeting.

Garcia and I finished up our dessert. On the way out of Martha's quaint establishment, I tipped my hat to Callahan. I think he still hadn't quite gotten over my boldness.

"I think we'll get along just fine, Ranger Dunn," chided Garcia as we parted company.

"I'll try to steer clear of your case, Arturo." I was careful not to address him as marshal. "Though I have a feeling we're chasing after some of the same folks. If I turn up anything, I'll get it to you."

Garcia nodded and headed up toward the railroad

camp. I saw him duck into an alley, emerging but moments later transformed from Deputy US Marshal Garcia to track-layer. He carried his professional wardrobe in a sack and now had donned dirty work pants, scuffed boots, and a sweat-stained shirt. I reckoned he was leading a charmed life.

THREE
POWERS THAT BE

I FOUND my mind dwelling on King Callahan. Logic told me to just write him off as a narcissist. In all my hanging with my dad around ranchers, I had not come upon him. Skidmore wasn't all that far from Nuecestown, so it bothered me that he'd been so close yet so far. I promised myself that I'd look into him after chatting with my old friend Archer Parr. It also didn't escape me that I needed to keep an eye out for Garth Jones. I sure didn't want to kill the man, as he seemed to be my only link to the next culprit up the power chain behind the killings.

I saddled and mounted Tornado, then headed south toward Archer Parr and the railroad town of Alice. Parr had been elected as a county commissioner. This was unsurprising given the rancher's proclivity toward people and politics. It was clear that he understood the importance of holding sway with the citizens. There was no question in my mind that Parr was destined for a political career of considerable power and commensurate influence. I reckoned to play to his outsized ego.

I didn't figure Parr to be directly connected with the

shenanigans surrounding the SP and the SA&AP, but I was betting on him knowing who might be involved. His growing connections with the movers and shakers in Austin was the subject of plenty of rumors.

Commercial farming and ranching developments in Texas benefitted from grants of more than thirty million acres that fueled their near-exponential growth. Railroads provided faster and cheaper transportation for people and products than most any other mode of transportation available. As a consequence of near-monopolistic rate and route controls contrived by the likes of moguls Jay Gould and Collis P. Huntington, and the growing complaints of mostly farmers and small businessmen, political debates flourished and government regulations followed. The Railroad Commission of Texas was founded to bring the Texas railroads to heel. Of course, the commission itself soon fell under the spell of politics and power.

I reckoned to tread lightly around this railroad power game, as it was a tad out of my league. My dad taught me that wisdom was the remedy for ignorance, arrogance, impatience, anger, and a bunch of other unsavory characteristics that usually got folks in trouble. The sum of life experiences—good and bad—formed the armor that was wisdom.

I actually wound up meeting Parr at a café in San Diego. I reckoned this was somewhat political, as the café was in Duval County. It was right next door to Alice on the border to Jim Wells County. Apparently, things had grown too warm for Parr in Jim Wells County.

Parr was seated toward the back of the café, where he could survey all the clientele as they came and went. They paid due homage of course. He offered me a cigar, which I graciously refused.

I waited patiently while Parr clipped and lit his cigar. No café patrons dared challenge him. The aroma of coffee would soon mix with cigar smoke.

Parr eyed me curiously as he took his initial pulls on the cigar. "Cuban? You sure?"

"Thanks kindly, but no," I reiterated.

"Haven't seen you in a while, Junior. Nice work on that Kerrville case. I'm sure Captain Hughes is right proud of you." He paused. "Your father, too."

I couldn't complain about Parr hanging plaudits on me. As I watched him blow cigar smoke toward the ceiling, I also couldn't help but realize that he wasn't much older than me but had taken a far different life path. From what I'd learned from my dad and seen in practice, corruption eventually reached its ugly claws out to men like Archer Parr. "Thanks, Archie. And congratulations on being elected county commissioner."

Parr offered a grateful nod at the recognition. "So, what's on your mind. Another tough case to crack?" His smile was ever-so-slightly patronizing, as though he knew that he always held a winning hand in the game of power. From what I gathered, all that saved me from Parr's arrogant intolerance was his growing respect for my accomplishments as a lawman.

"Captain Hughes has me working on a couple of murders up near Skidmore on that railroad that Uriah Lott sold to the Southern Pacific." I saw that I had grabbed his interest at the mention of Lott. "There's a crew building a siding. Two teamsters were killed in broad daylight. I think I know who the killer is, but I'm looking to bring to justice whoever paid the killer."

Parr had taken a long pull on the cigar and coughed at

my saying that I might know the killer. He quickly gathered his wits. "The money behind this isn't in Texas, Junior. We're talking seriously big money."

"Washington, DC?" I ventured.

Parr chuckled. "Bigger than that, Junior. Those chiselers in the nation's capital couldn't begin to grasp the stakes."

"Gould family?" I knew that Jay Gould had passed from consumption only five years ago, but his family money still ran deep in Texas railroads.

Parr chuckled. "Old man Gould is dead, and his family isn't exactly interested in Texas goings on. This reeks of Southern Pacific interests."

"Huntington?"

"Likely powers that are associated with him. He's growing long of tooth, Junior. His mind is sharp, but he's getting on in years." Parr paused as though for effect and blew smoke upward. "You can't touch Huntington anyway. He lives up in New York and occasionally travels to California. If I were you, I'd be looking at the Railroad Commission of Texas." He took another pull on his smoke. "You hear of a fellow named Callahan?"

I braced a bit at that. "This Callahan involved?"

"I hear tell he's got money coming from somewhere. Might be connected." Parr gave me a knowing expression.

I felt as though Parr was holding something back but decided not to press him. In a bizarre sort of way, I had to protect his backside. He could honestly tell any inquiring folks that he told me nothing of what Callahan might be up to. "I'm much obliged for your perspective, Archie."

Parr stood as a way of dismissing me. "You get a chance, you might get yourself up near Waco. A fellow named William Crush, who works for the Missouri-Kansas-Texas Railroad, is cooking up plans to stage a locomotive crash in September. It should be quite a spectacle."

The image of two iron horses plowing into each other sounded dumber than knocking rocks together. It sounded like a major waste of two locomotives. Nevertheless, I couldn't help but feel curious. I made a note to myself to wander up to Waco near the middle of September.

I was less than a day's ride from Nuecestown and Heaven's Gate Ranch. I dared not be so close and not visit my wife. Cassie would swoon with delight. I reckoned I could use a great meal and her loving ways...not necessarily in that order. More importantly, she was pregnant, and I wanted to be at home for the blessed event.

Tornado quickly caught on to where we were headed. He likely got to thinking on a mare or two to get reacquainted with.

The ride was uneventful, though I was always mindful that the likes of Garth Jones could be lurking. I didn't especially relish the prospect of any confrontation, and that's what it would likely be. The likes of Jones with vengeance on their minds wouldn't resort to bushwhacking. They'd want to be certain you knew who was seeking their own brand of retribution.

Long about midday, Tornado's ears perked up and nostrils flared. It was all I could do to hold him back as we rode through the gateway arch of Heaven's Gate Ranch.

I reined in about fifty yards shy of the house. Cassie was on her knees tending to the flower bed across the front of the gallery. I had to admit that her flowers were right pretty. Little Sean was playing in the dirt nearby. I was fixing to sneak up on her when a mare in the corral whinnied and Tornado echoed her call.

Cassie glanced at the corral, then over her shoulder at

me. "Lucas!" She got up and ran to me as fast as a very pregnant woman can run.

I barely had time to dismount, as she leaped into my arms.

She buried her face in my chest.

I grabbed her shoulders, held her at arm's length, and laid loving eyes upon her. "How much longer?"

"Any day, love. I'm so happy you're here."

Sean toddled over and wrapped himself around my leg. It was as though he was laying claim to his turf. I tousled his hair and hoisted him high. I got to thinking about how my dad had been away a lot when I was growing up. He was around just enough to forge bonds with me and my brothers and sisters, but he spent many weeks away from home on the trail of lawbreakers. "I sure missed y'all."

"It's about noon, Lucas. Come on in, and I'll feed my men."

With Sean on my hip, I followed Cassie into the kitchen. She sure had it fixed up right nice. It was decidedly well-equipped; likely the influence of our mothers. I sat at the table and played hand games with Sean.

"How's the case in Skidmore going?" asked Cassie.

I dreaded having to mention Garth Jones. "I'm making progress. There's big railroad money and political power at work."

"What about the killings?"

"Looks like a paid killer."

"Any idea who?" she pressed.

"Witness accounts point to Garth Jones," I said reluctantly. I saw Cassie's shoulders tense as she cut vegetables. "I'm trying to avoid a confrontation. I'd like to capture Jones and find out who hired him."

Cassie dropped the cutting knife and walked over to the

cupboard. She gathered a stack of papers and dropped it in front of me.

I eased Sean to the floor and perused the papers one at a time. There must have been thirty of them. Each was a threat written in Garth Jones' tell-tale script. "I'm sorry you've had to endure this," I lamented. What else could I say? What evil possessed Jones' vile mind that he would terrorize my wife? I tore up the notes. I could destroy them, but not the messages.

Cassie returned to fixing our meal. It was as close to normalcy as she could muster for the moment.

"I reckon to be here for a bit, sweetheart. The Ranger business I have is close at hand." I felt guilty at the prospect of being away at our second child's birth, but this was not the time for me to be absent from Cassie.

"Double," demanded the black-clad figure.

"That's a lot of money," retorted the voice from the night shadows.

"You want me to eliminate two men, and one a Texas Ranger." The words came out matter-of-factly. The word eliminate was a sorry substitute for murder. Garth Jones didn't mind bushwhacking the tracklayer but had in mind a confrontation with the Texas Ranger. That would be dangerous. "Ten thousand each. Half up front, same as before. Take it or leave it."

The deep voice in the shadows was silent.

"What's your pleasure?"

"Don't waste any time." A sack of gold coins was passed in the dimness of the night. Only the stars bore witness.

FOUR
BAD ANSWERS

CASSIE MAY HAVE BEEN ready to burst with child, but she didn't hold back in our bed. I had to compensate for the past couple of weeks of my traipsing around central Texas. Not that I minded. We'd opened a bottle of wine fermented from our own orchard. It gave an atmosphere of romance to what was a fully carnal act.

Her lips explored every inch of my body. Her hands paused at the scars from past bullet wounds, as though reliving how close she's come to losing me. That seemed to arouse her to a desperate passion.

I wasn't holding back. Her belly had an enticing effect on me. My lips explored her nether region, then found their way to her swollen breasts. It wasn't until these moments of unbridled passion that I realized how very much I missed our intimacy. Our passions were rising to a fever pitch.

Cassie pushed me onto my back and mounted me. She teased for but a moment before consuming me in her fire. Ecstasy. This was heaven on earth.

Our passions spent; we lay back. She perspired. I sweated. She nestled under my arm.

After our lovemaking, we gravitated to the gallery to relax. We enjoyed a light breeze as we cooled off from our ardor. Folks say absence makes the heart grow fonder. It was a tad more than that for Cassie and me. Well, a good bit more than a tad. As we sipped the last of the wine from earlier, a young boy on a fine gelding galloped up to the house.

The boy reined in before us and pulled an envelope from his saddlebag. "I was asked to personally deliver this to Texas Ranger Lucas Dunn, Junior. Are you him?"

I smiled and nodded. "That I am, son."

He stretched high in his saddle and handed me the note.

I went to fetch a coin from my pocket.

"I've been well paid, sir," said the boy in refusing my money. With that, he turned and rode off.

I shrugged and turned to Cassie. My gut told me what was inside the envelope.

"Looks like some other envelopes," advised Cassie.

I tore it open and slowly unfolded the note. This one raised my eyebrows.

"What's it say?" asked Cassie.

I handed the note to her. A single word was scribbled across the paper, *Tomorrow*. It sent an involuntary chill coursing up my spine. Jones intended to confront me. When? Where?

Morning broke on a slightly cooler day. Cassie gave me *the look* as I strapped on my holster with the Smith & Wesson revolver and headed to the barn. She was understandably worried. I reckoned to curry Tornado and clean the stalls. Turned out that our ranch hands had already mucked and spread fresh hay. I strolled over to Tornado and stroked his snout while offering a sugar cube. He was right pleased with that.

"You're lucky, Tornado old boy." I chuckled. He had that look in his eyes. The look that asks to turn him to those mares he'd seen when we rode in. He nickered and whinnied aplenty as I led him out of the barn and cut him loose in the west pasture. At least three mares perked up upon seeing him galloping toward them. Go figure.

"Ranger Dunn," came the deep voice behind me.

"Captain?" I turned to face Captain Hughes.

"Good thing I was no lawbreaker seeking vengeance, Junior. Didn't you hear our hosses?"

I'd been so focused on Tornado that I'd been careless. "You don't know the half of it, Captain." We shook hands.

"We were up in San Antonio and heading back to the Rio Grande. Figured I'd see whether you and your dad might be around. How's the Skidmore case going?"

I debated as to whether to tell him about the Deputy US Marshal, but reckoned it was best to be straight. If he learned about it later, it would have broken a trust. "I'm sure who committed the killings, but figure to find out who's paying the hired gun. There's a small complication, as there's an undercover Deputy US Marshal investigating the Southern Pacific's dealings with the Railroad Commission of Texas. I've met him and promised to avoid messing with his doings."

Hughes nodded. "What haven't you told me?"

Dang, but the captain was wily as a fox.

"Got a threatening note yesterday from the killer," I responded.

"Sounds personal, Junior," observed Hughes.

I sighed. "I pursued him months back in connection

with the Kerrville murders. I wounded him, and he's determined to confront me."

"Guess you're not worried," temporized the captain with a rye grin.

I smiled sheepishly. He'd snuck up behind me far too easily. "I'll be careful. I sure don't reckon on one of those gunfights the dime-store novels used to talk about. I'm no Wild Bill Hickock or John Wesley Hardin. Besides, I want to capture him and find out whose payroll he's on. His name is Garth Jones. He's a swarthy black-clad character with a mangled right hand from one of my bullets."

Hughes nodded. "Well, my men are getting restless at me jawing here with you, Junior. They have enjoyed the coffee your wife served up, the bear sign, too. She's a mighty fine hostess, and you're looking to be a father again. All the more reason for you to be especially careful. If we see your man, we'll see what we can do to corral him, but we're running a bit late. The men want a night in Corpus Christi before we head south." Hughes shrugged. "I'm sure you have this well in hand, Ranger."

We shook hands. Hughes joined his men and rode out.

I wasn't sure what to make of his action or, more accurately, inaction. It would have been great to have a passel of Texas Rangers around for a couple of days, but then Jones might never have shown up. It was just as well that he continued his mission. It was also a sign of his confidence in me that I had this case under control.

With Tornado having his way with the mares, I headed back to the big house. Maybe Cassie would still have some hot coffee and those delicious bear sign treats.

★★

"Susanna Sparks is coming by today, Lucas. She's figuring that I'm about due and wants to be around to help. She may stay a few nights until the birth."

I felt relieved, as I didn't feature having to handle child birthing duties. "That's right generous of Susanna," I observed with a tone of relief.

"Men," teased Cassie with a swish of her skirt.

"Your man is here for you, sweetheart."

"Your Texas Ranger friends were right polite," she mused. "Gave me a more secure feeling to have them around." She knew full well that they weren't coming back.

I caught her implication. She was worried sick. "The day's not half done, sweetheart." How might Jones approach me? I truly wanted to capture him. I sure didn't feature being the loser in any facedown. Then it struck me. I needed to be the aggressor. It was like back on the Guadalupe River, when I snuck up on him as he lay in ambush to bushwhack me. Importantly, this was my home turf, and I knew it like the back of my hand. "I've got to go do what I must do, Cassie." We kissed, and I headed out.

I grabbed my Winchester, checked the loads in the Smith & Wesson, and headed out. Importantly, I swapped out my boots and spurs for a pair of moccasins and donned a buck-skin shirt to better blend with the natural cover. This task would be undertaken on foot. Tornado could entertain his mares to his heart's content. If all worked out, we'd take a ride tomorrow—or maybe escort a prisoner to the Nueces-town jail.

I headed off into the woods a hundred yards or so from the big house. I passed the one-room log cabin that had been my folks' first home out here on the Texas Nueces Strip. I looked back at the big house that we now occupied and thought of the house they now lived in but a few miles off. My dad oversaw one of the largest spreads in Texas and

Heaven's Gate Ranch wasn't far behind. Wasn't bad for a family of Irish immigrants. Folks back in County Kildare would have been proud of them.

There it was. My dad had built the tree stand many years back. It was nearly impossible for the unpracticed eye to see it. Many a deer had met its fate from one of us staked out in its lofty perch among the tree branches. From this place, I could surveil a wide swath of the area around the big house and deep into the surrounding woods. I figured it would be the logical route for Jones to use as his approach.

I climbed up. From this vantage point, I could see the big house. If Jones appeared, it was highly probable that I'd spot him. The irony of this place wasn't lost on me, as I could see the spot where Jones stood as my bullet mangled his hand. It was just a few months back.

Off in the distant corral alongside the barn, I saw Tornado whinny and prance about. He wasn't excited about mares. My keen eyes scanned the area around the corral. Nothing.

It occurred to me that we needed a dog. Sean would love having a companion, and the critter would be around to warn of intruders. I made a mental note to follow up on that.

As I glanced down to recheck the load in my carbine, I caught a shadowy movement in the woods near the corral. "Well, I'll be," I murmured.

Garth Jones was leaning his lithe black-clad form behind a live oak.

I smiled. He looked to be trying to decide his next move. He'd arrived at Heaven's Gate but seemed uncertain as to how to get to me. He looked over at the bunkhouse. He couldn't be too careful, as we did have a couple of cowhands. Luckily for Jones, they were chasing mavericks far out on one of our pastures.

The bold thing for him to do would be to call me out. Of course, that would also be stupid. We could hole up in the big house for weeks. Moreover, when our cowhands returned, Jones would be vulnerable. If shots were fired, it wouldn't take long to raise most of the folks hither and yon to corral the outlaw.

Now that I had Jones spotted, I reckoned I could safely slip from the tree and make my way behind him. There was a dry streambed behind him with plenty of brush that would cover my approach. My stealthy hunting skills honed over many hunts with my dad figured to serve me in good stead. I'd successfully snuck up on the outlaw before and was confident that I could do it again.

Jones was focused on the house and trying to decide his next move, as I quietly slipped from the tree stand. I permitted myself a smirk. This was looking to be far too easy.

A light rain last night helped muffle any noise I might make. Wearing moccasins had certainly been a great choice. It took a mere fifteen minutes to find my way to the arroyo and then worm my way to a position only twenty or so feet behind Jones. He was clueless as to my presence.

His body language told me that he was about to make a move. He scribbled something on a piece of paper.

I shook my head. He appeared as though he was going to leave another one of his damnable notes. It was time to act. "Garth Jones, drop your gun, step away from the tree, and grab sky." My voice seemed even more commanding in the heavy, humid air.

Jones froze. Once again, I'd snuck up on his sorry butt. He leaned the carbine against the tree and stepped away. He simultaneously released the tie on the Colt in his holster.

I didn't miss that move. Would he be so stupid as to try a move while staring down the muzzle of my Winchester? "What now, Mr. Ranger?" he challenged.

"You're under arrest for murder, Mr. Jones." I moved toward him and grabbed the handcuffs from my belt pouch.

"You taking me in all by yourself?" Jones' tone was hardly one of respect.

I had the urge to pop him up the side of his head with my fist. Lord knows, I was bigger and stronger than he. I didn't even know whether he was necessarily meaner. "That's exactly what I'm fixing to do." I caught a squint in his eye, as though he was deciding to go for the Colt nestled so temptingly in his holster. "Don't be stupid. Back away from the tree." Jones backed away and I placed the rifle well out of his reach. "Now place your feet apart and lean against the tree with your hands high."

Jones sighed and did as told.

I relieved him of the Colt and cuffed him. "Let's head over to yonder barn and have us a conversation."

"You going to talk me to death, Mr. Ranger?" snarled Jones. He was none too happy with his situation.

"Just get moving," I demanded.

We reached the barn, and I ordered Jones to sit on a bench just inside the door. He sat and gave me a quizzical eye. I leaned the Winchester well beyond reach and drew my Bowie knife. "I need some information," I said with as diabolical a smile as I could muster.

Jones' eyes widened at seeing the razor-sharp blade.

"Last time we met here, I had an old friend with me name of Buffalo Watts. He was one of the very last of the mountain men." I paused for effect, as I made a show of testing the knife edge. "You might call him a close family friend. Watts used to tell us tales of what the Indians did to their captives. Can't say as I've had much practice at those methods, so forgive me if I mess up. I'll try to keep blood loss to a minimum."

The look on Jones' face was priceless. "You wouldn't. You can't. It's illegal," he began to plead.

I'd convinced him that I was deadly serious. "Who paid you to kill the teamsters?" I asked calmly.

"I don't know," replied Jones.

I made a show of a fake sigh. "This can be easy or difficult for you. Who paid you?" I repeated.

Jones struggled with the cuffs. "I'm telling you I don't know. Never saw a face or heard a name."

"Shall we begin with an ear?" I threatened. As I brought the knife close, he tried to duck. "Don't be having me make a mess with this here Bowie knife. Just hold still and take it like a man."

"I'm telling you, I don't know!" he screamed. If he was lying, it was a hell of a convincing lie.

I pulled back the knife and gave him a long, hard look. I believed he was telling the truth. He honestly didn't know who had hired him. This was not helpful. "A voice?"

Jones' nod was accompanied by a sigh of relief. "Deep voice. Male."

"Make out anything? Big man?" I asked.

"Shadows. Hard to tell. Might have been big, but not so big as you." He responded.

"Anything else? How did he pay you? A bank?"

"Paid in gold coin. I rightly appreciated that," said Jones with a smile.

"Where did you meet?" I pressed.

"In the woods about a mile north of Skidmore," he replied.

"He paying you to shoot anyone else?"

Jones gave me a long, hard look as if trying to decide

how much he could or should reveal. "What you going to do with me after this...this talk?"

"Jail in Nuecestown for the present. Now, are you to shoot anyone else?"

"Some nigah working the tracklaying crew."

Holy smoke! He was being hired to kill Garcia. The marshal's cover had been blown. "Do you know who your victim on the crew is?"

"Didn't give no name. Just that he was a darky and where I could find him. I didn't do it yet."

I breathed a sigh of relief at that. "That man is a Deputy US Marshal. You'd have committed a federal offense, Jones."

Jones' mouth gaped a tad. "Damn."

If there was any sort of honor among outlaws, Jones might have had a tiny bit of it. "What's on the note?"

Jones laughed. "I was going to tell you I'd get you somewhere else. I couldn't figure how to get you out in the open."

"You know, I'm sorry about your hand. Things like that can happen when folks are shooting at each other." I tried to be compassionate. "You could've been killed." I realized that was little comfort for a man with a badly crippled hand.

He gave me a long, hard look. "Can't be forgiving that, Mr. Texas Ranger."

Unsaid was that I'd embarrassed him several times, from discovering him spying on me to sneaking up on him to wounding and now capturing him. I'd become his archnemesis. "Well, let's head to Nuecestown," I urged matter-of-factly. "Where's your hoss?"

Jones nodded to a thicket beyond the corral. "Damn cayuse stirred up that stallion in the corral."

I shook my head. It always seemed that lawbreakers

eventually did stupid things. In Jones' case, he was going to attack me on my own turf. "Well, you don't move a muscle, while I saddle up." Just in case, I tied a tether to the cuffs behind Jones' back and tied it to a post.

I fetched Tornado, saddled up, and led him and Jones from the barn to get his horse. Given how lean he was, it was no trouble to lift him into the saddle. Once mounted, I led the way to the front of the big house. Cassie saw me coming and stepped out onto the gallery.

"I'll be back in the morning. I've got to lock this rascal up." The ride to Nuecestown took nearly a day, so I reckoned to spend the night. "I'll take Mr. Jones here to Corpus Christi and place him in Sheriff McTiernan's care to hold for trial."

I blew Cassie a kiss and headed out with Jones seated on his horse towed on a long tether.

The night at the Nuecestown jail went about as well as expected. The town was dying owing to the railroad having passed it by. It was an economic thing. They had a one-room schoolhouse, but I reckoned that facility and the cemetery would eventually be all that remained. Anyway, the jail had not been kept up very well, but it sufficed as shelter for the night. The toughest part of my duty was guarding Jones while he answered nature's call.

Jones and I had nothing to say on the next morning on our ride into Corpus Christi. We reined in at Sheriff McTiernan's office. I glanced at Jones as I dismounted. He seemed pretty much resigned to his fate. Technically, I'd solved the crime by arresting him and bringing him in, though I found myself haunted by the mystery over who was behind Jones' deeds.

I knocked on McTiernan's door.

"Yep. Who's there and what do y'all want?" came the reply. It seemed decidedly un-sheriff-like to me.

"It's me; Texas Ranger Lucas Dunn. Come on out and take this prisoner off my hands, John."

The door creaked open, and I found myself staring into the half-awake eyes of one of McTiernan's deputies. "Whatcha want?" he droned.

"Is Sheriff McTiernan around?"

"He be off eatin'," responded the deputy. He spat from the tobacco quid stuffed between his cheek and gum. It narrowly missed my foot. "Yuh say yer a Ranger?"

"Please fetch Sheriff McTiernan. He knows me. I will be leaving this here prisoner in your jail to be held over for trial. He's charged with two murders."

Jones heard the conversation and couldn't help but crack a smile. Sizing up the deputy, he surely had to feel confident that he could find some way to escape.

"I don't fetch fer nobody."

I couldn't help myself. I grabbed the deputy by the shirt collar and lifted him off his feet. "Don't you ever sass me, deputy. You go and fetch Sheriff McTiernan."

As he was released, the deputy accidentally swallowed his chaw. He choked for a moment, then recovered. "Y-y-yessir," he stammered and ran off toward a restaurant up the street.

Soon, McTiernan came striding up the street with the apologetic yammering deputy falling all over himself behind him. "What's up, Junior?" he called out as he neared me.

"I'd be pleased to leave Mr. Garth Jones here in your capable hands to await trial, Sheriff. He's charged with two murders in Skidmore."

"You know that's out of my jurisdiction," responded McTiernan.

"Not a jurisdiction concern. This is a Texas matter and possibly federal."

McTiernan nodded. "Deputy, escort Mr. Jones here to a cell."

The deputy shrugged, looked at the sheriff and me, and eased Jones from his horse.

"When you have him locked up, you can return those handcuffs to me, deputy." I handed the key to the deputy and turned to McTiernan. "Let's get the paperwork begun, John. I aim to get back to Heaven's Gate before nightfall and then must head on to Skidmore." I followed the sheriff to his office, while the deputy headed Jones off to a cell.

"Why you headed back to Skidmore if you captured the killer, Junior?" asked McTiernan.

"I've got to contact Captain Hughes, but there's more to the case than murder. I aim to track down whoever paid Jones," I replied. I likely said too much but trusted the sheriff.

I'd just sat down when a ruckus came from back among the jail cells. I drew my Smith & Wesson and hauled ass in the direction of the fracas.

Jones stood over the deputy. He had the deputy's gun in his good hand, had pulled back the hammer, and was aiming at the hapless deputy's head. My handcuffs hung from the wrist of his mangled right hand.

"You put up that gun, Jones, or you're a dead man," I snarled. A .44 caliber slug at close range would put a whale of a hole through Jones' chest, and he knew it.

Jones looked beneath him at the cowering deputy and then stared down the barrel of my gun.

Sheriff McTiernan appeared beside me with a 10-gauge

sawed-off shotgun. Any wrong move by Jones would be ugly.

"You looking to put another murder on the court docket, Garth? Put it up." I demanded.

Jones sighed, spat, and dropped the deputy's gun. "Damn!" he uttered resignedly.

I grabbed Jones by the neck, nearly lifting him off the floor. "You ever come near my family again, I will kill you." I couldn't have been any clearer. "Now, get your sorry ass into that cell," I directed.

The deputy pulled himself up off the floor, relieved Jones of the handcuffs, and gave him an extra nudge into the cell before closing and locking the door.

McTiernan and I looked at each other and shook our heads. "You're going to have to keep an eye on that one, John," I noted.

McTiernan chuckled as we headed back to his office. "Jones or my deputy," he joked.

Soon enough, I found myself headed home.

FIVE
DETECTIVE WORK

WELL, I sure didn't have much to go on. As Tornado and I plodded along, I reckoned to hang at Heaven's Gate for another day before heading back to Skidmore. I did need to warn Garcia that he'd been discovered. I was also curious as to who in the region might be of fair size and have a deep voice, along with the power to order up murder.

Upon pausing at the gateway arch to Heaven's Gate, I reflected a bit. Decision made, I turned Tornado toward Nuecestown. It wasn't long before I'd pulled up at the blacksmith shop. The smithy was banging away on a glowing piece of steel that would soon become a branding iron.

"Yo, Zeke!" I hollered.

Zeke paused as though he'd thought he'd heard something between hammer bangs in the anvil. He looked around and finally spotted me. "Junior, what brings you here? Horse need a shoe?" His smile acknowledged the many times he'd come out to Heaven's Gate to shoe horses or fix just about anything iron.

"You still have them pups? You know; the ones they call the Blue Lacy breed?"

Zeke smiled. "Matter of fact, I've got two of the little critters, Junior. You interested?"

I thought a moment. I wanted to bring home a dog for Sean. Did I want two?

"Matched set, Junior; a male and a female. Right purty."

The Blue Lacy had been bred by four brothers in Kerrville to herd hogs. They supposedly mixed greyhounds, scent hounds, and coyotes, though I'd heard that wolves were also bred into the mix. The Blue Lacy dogs were supposed to be great family dogs and hard workers, even herding cattle. I dismounted and ambled over to a fenced area alongside the smithy shop.

"Ten bucks, and they're yours," offered Zeke, as he wiped sooty sweat from his forehead with a heavily-muscled forearm.

"Seven?" I countered.

Zeke extended his massive paw. "They're yours."

Now, I had to transport two squirmy pups to the ranch.

Zeke gave a broad smile as though reading my mind. "I'll throw in a couple of collars. Give'em long leashes, and they'll be just fine."

Tornado and I were back on the road soon with two exceptionally playful puppies in tow. Upon reaching the barn, I rode straight on in with the pups. I tied off their leashes to a post. I could hardly contain myself as I thought of seeing Sean's reaction. After currying Tornado and letting him to pasture, I headed to the big house. I had noted Susanna Sparks' horse in the barn and her buggy parked outside. That she was still here should have been a hint, but the puppies wouldn't let me consider the meaning of her ongoing presence.

Filled with curiosity, I quietly entered the house. My legs were immediately grabbed in a bear hug by Sean. "Shhhh," I cautioned and picked him up. "What's happening?"

Sean spied the two dogs and let out a joyful squeal. He squirmed from my grasp and fell in among his new playmates. The expression on his face was as only two-year-old little boys with nary a clue about life can offer. His world had just been filled with new adventure.

"Where's Momma?" I asked.

With arms draped around the puppies, he looked up the stairs with a mischievous smile as though holding a secret.

"Let's go see." I took his hand and headed up the stairs. The puppies followed. I somehow managed to get to the bedroom door without arousing attention. As I reached for the handle, the door swung open and Susanna Sparks gave a start.

Cassie lay asleep on our bed with a bundle nestled beside her.

"Congratulations, Lucas Dunn. You've got another son," whispered Sparks. She glanced down at the puppies. "They'd best not come in here."

Sean squealed with delight, and that was enough to awaken Cassie. She turned her head lazily toward me and smiled. "We need a name, Mr. Texas Ranger," she half-whispered as the bundle stirred.

Sparks threw up her hands, grabbed the puppy's leashes, and headed downstairs. "I'm going to brew some coffee," she called out. "And teach these pups some manners," she added with a laugh.

I strode over to the bed. The bundle had come alive and

now suckled at Cassie's breast. "You name him, sweetheart," I said.

Cassie smiled as though hoping I'd say that. "Bode," she said. It had been her beloved but rascally grandfather's name.

"Bode it is," I replied and gave her a long kiss. I brushed my lips gently on Bode's head as he nursed. "Welcome to the family, Bode."

"Did all go well?" asked Cassie. "And what was that commotion outside the bedroom?"

I nodded. "Figure to let Captain Hughes know what's happened and then head up to Skidmore to warn Garcia. I'll hang around here for a few days until..."

Cassie interrupted. "Until I'm strong enough?" she challenged.

I had tread on tenuous ground. Cassie was ever the strong Texas frontier-seasoned wife. "Just to spend time with you, Bode, and Sean, sweetheart." I tried to recover.

She smiled. If ever a smile could light up a room, it was Cassie's. "Did I hear dogs?"

"Sure enough." It occurred to me that I hadn't named the little critters. "Got a couple of Blue Lacy pups from Zeke back in Nuecestown. Figured Sean would love them to death."

"They have names?"

My mind had been tripping through possible names. "Thought we might call them Brody and Tess."

Cassie smiled. "Good as any, Lucas. I sort of like the names," she half-whispered. She was getting sleepy.

"Daddy?" Sean interrupted. "I eat?"

"Susanna will feed you both. I'll be up and around by tomorrow," Cassie assured me.

"I love you," I said with moistened eyes.

"I know. Now, git. I need sleep."

This was the sort of circumstance that caused me to rethink my commitment to being a lawman. I know that my dad dealt with it, and I suspected that many men behind the badge did.

It was especially tough to leave Cassie. She amazed me at how quickly she was back up and doing all she had to do around our home. Seemed that half the time baby Bode was at a breast while Sean split time between hanging onto one of us. One of these days, the boys would be old enough to go hunting and fishing. I didn't wish them a lawman's life, but wouldn't discourage them from it either.

"I don't figure to be in Skidmore but a few days, sweetheart," I said from atop Tornado. I hadn't heard back from Captain Hughes as to whether I should dig deeper into the money behind the killings. Would jailing the killer be enough to satisfy the powers that be? I sure was curious as to who paid Garth Jones.

Four days had passed since leaving Jones residing in a jail cell in Corpus Christi. I figured Garcia was at least temporarily out of danger.

As I rode through the gateway to our ranch, a lone rider approached on a well-lathered horse. He appeared to be unarmed, though I did loosen the tie holding my Smith & Wesson in its holster.

"Mr. Dunn! Mr. Dunn!" called the rider, waving an envelope over his head. It was all he could do to rein in without running into me and Tornado.

"Whoa! Easy does it," I cautioned. "What's your hurry?"

The rider struggled to catch his breath. "Got a message fer yuh," he managed. He handed the envelope to me.

I wondered whether folks had heard of the telephone. It was a lot easier on horseflesh. I flipped a coin to the courier and tore open the envelope. It was a telegram from Captain Hughes.

TEXAS RANGER LUCAS DUNN, JR
  D COMPANY, FRONTIER BATTALION
  NUECESTOWN, TEXAS

CLEAR TO PURSUE TRC CASE.

CAPTAIN JOHN R HUGHES
  D COMPANY, FRONTIER BATTALION
  TEXAS RANGERS
  BROWNSVILLE, TEXAS

Well, that was clear enough for me. It was purposely designed to be cryptic to others. Hughes was telling me to check out the Railroad Commission of Texas and seek the money behind the attack on the SA&AP Railroad.

The courier turned his horse, then paused. "Mr. Dunn?" he asked tentatively.

"Yes?"

"Sheriff said to keep it quiet, but some prizner busted outta the jail. Deputy got kilt." He gave me a frightened look, as though telling too much, and spurred off.

I was left sitting astride Tornado with my mouth agape. Couldn't McTiernan hold his man? "Come on, Tornado, let's ride." Off we went at a canter. I'd have to give my trusty steed a break, but I felt we needed to hustle to Skidmore. If Jones was on the loose, Garcia was in danger. I wished there was a way to reach him sooner, but I had no idea what name he might be using as cover. I regretted not finding out when we'd met over dinner. In any case, I had to reach Skidmore as fast as Tornado's legs could carry us.

Dusk had settled by the time I pulled up at Jenkins' tent.

Jenkins was busy swatting mosquitoes, as he closed for the evening. He looked up, as I reined in.

"You're late, Texas Ranger," he announced.

I gave him an inquisitive look.

"Damn bushwhacker killed one of my tracklayers. A greaser," he lamented.

Had I arrived too late? Had Garth Jones already struck?

"Damn fool was standing next to one of those other greasers."

"Which one was shot?" I pressed.

"No matter. They work hard. But you know…they all look alike." Jenkins shook his head as if revealing some great piece of knowledge about Mexicans. "Body is behind the general store waiting for a box."

"One survived?" I asked.

"Yeah, but he got winged by a second shot. We carted him off to the doc. No sense letting good labor bleed out."

"Where is the doctor's place?"

"In town. Sign out front. Can't miss it." Jenkins caught my deep concern. "What brung you back to Skidmore, Ranger? Heard tell you got the man who killed the teamsters."

I shook my head. "I'm heading to the doctor's place. I'll tell you more tomorrow." I figured to find out exactly who had been shot before jumping to any conclusions. I bid

Jenkins goodbye, vaulted back into my saddle, and headed to town. All the way, I prayed that the dead man wasn't Garcia.

I stopped at the general store first. Blessedly, the body of this victim wasn't Garcia.

Somewhat reassured, I headed off to find the doctor. His office was hard to miss, as his sign listed a multitude of ailments he dealt with, including removing bullets. He appeared to have a sense of humor. I hitched Tornado, strode to the doctor's front door, and knocked loudly.

"Hold on, doggone it! I'm coming!" came the voice from within. In but a moment, the door swung wide open, and a gray-haired man of short stature and pleasant expression greeted me. "You in a hurry? You hurt?"

"Sorry. I'm Texas Ranger Lucas Dunn. I learned from Mr. Jenkins that you are treating a gunshot victim here."

"I'm Doc Coltrane. Pleased to make your acquaintance. I did treat a Mexican man suffering from a gunshot wound. He's not here." Doc Coltrane motioned up the street. "I think the man might be at the livery. His wound was serious but not life-threatening." Coltrane paused. "You working a case?"

"Do you have his name?" I asked.

He shook his head. "Never do ask when I treat gunshot wounds. Keeps me out of trouble."

I sighed. What sort of doctor treats a man and doesn't get his name? There was likely something illegal about it, but that wasn't my concern. "I'm after the shooter, doc. Thanks kindly." I bade farewell, grabbed Tornado's reins, and headed for the livery stable.

The stable boy greeted me. "Need yer hoss stabled, mistuh?"

I ignored his question. "You have a Mexican here?"

"You mean the greaser? He be in a stall back thar." He pointed straight back to a stall in the rear.

I pushed past him and headed for the stall he'd pointed to and peered inside. The man was not Arturo Garcia. I was much relieved. Now, I had to reach Garcia before the killer figured he'd shot the wrong men. Killer? Was Garth Jones back in action? I cursed under my breath. I was done with capturing the damned outlaw. Next time we met, he'd be on the receiving end of a slug from my gun.

I was more determined than ever to meet King Callahan and have a conversation. I thought back to the time a few weeks back when we'd met at Martha's restaurant. He wasn't a huge man, but he was big enough to qualify from what Jones had described. Deep voice? I didn't really recall, other than that it had an air of command to it.

Come morning, I headed to Jenkins' tent.

He was briskly fanning himself while reviewing a bill of lading. "Morning, Ranger," he said matter-of-factly as though anxious for his work and its associated worries needed to be put far behind him.

"Good morning, Mr. Jenkins. Mind if I talk to some of your crew? I'm interested in finding witnesses to those latest killings."

"Help yourself. Another two weeks and we'll be done here. Can't happen soon enough," he assured me.

It didn't take me long to spot Garcia working up a sweat, pounding a rail spike. I questioned a couple of tracklayers along the way just to seem proper. I finally reached Garcia. "Got a minute?" I asked with just a hint of urgency.

We walked over to a nearby water bucket. He nonchalantly picked up a ladle and took a drink.

"Your cover has been broken. The bullets yesterday were meant for you," I advised.

"How do you know this?" pressed Garcia.

"I learned it from the man someone is paying to stop the Southern Pacific. They hired him to kill me, too, but I knew his habits and turned the tables on him."

Garcia hung his head. "Thanks. Guess it's time for action."

I looked at him inquisitively.

He laughed. "You talked to King Callahan yet?"

"Why? Have you?" I pressed.

"Don't figure to, but I figured I'd toss the suggestion out to you. My prey is far bigger than him." Garcia began walking toward the tent where he stowed his tracklayer duds.

"You said it was time for action," I said as I followed.

"Can't say much about it." Garcia shook his head ruefully. "Sorry. I'm not sure how much you know about the Railroad Commission of Texas. It's an agency that doesn't actually have much direct clout. It has neither the authority to set rates nor the resources to conduct court battles. But it has influence nevertheless. Former Texas Lieutenant Governor Leonidas Storey was recently appointed by Governor Hogg to head the commission. Storey has been faced with declining freight rates that make it difficult for the railroads to upgrade their equipment. The result is a gradual decline in service and degradation of infrastructure. Big money folks are looking to watch the value of the properties drop then snap them up for a fraction of their true worth. My challenge is to root out who is doing what to whom."

That was about as long a mouthful as I'd yet heard from Arturo Garcia. It demanded a broader explanation, but I figured I wouldn't be hearing more today. I gathered that somewhere in the mix among the likes of Callahan and Storey, the railroad moguls, and the political powers-that-be laid an intricately woven web.

The justice business can be frustrating to work within. Sheriffs have their county jurisdictions, US Marshals deal with federal matters, and the Texas Rangers have state responsibilities. Cooperation among the agencies was spotty at best. Garcia and I had already shared more than most. Still, I didn't understand why he had logged his presence at the Huntsville prison and was posing as a track-layer. It made no sense, unless he was trying to shake any perceived association with the US Marshals. Something greater had to be afoot. "Well, good luck, Arturo. Do watch out for that bushwhacker. I'm sure he hasn't given up." I reckoned the warning stood for me as well.

Garth Jones lurked out there somewhere. After running afoul of me, he must have figured that Garcia would be the easier man to kill. Then, he obviously had trouble identifying his target. My experience told me that he'd received some portion of his fee in advance. He had yet to earn the balance and must be frustrated. After all, his reputation was on the line. I instinctively scanned the area as I left Garcia's company. It was time to have a talk with King Callahan.

"I need more," pleaded Jones.

"You haven't even delivered one," replied the voice in

the shadows. "You're littering Texas with bodies, but not the ones that I'm paying you to kill."

"It's not been so easy as I figured," insisted Jones.

"Damn. You missing them has them extra cautious. It's not going to be any easier. This isn't a game." There was a long silence. "Tell you what. Kill one, and I'll give you a tad more of the balance. If it's the fed, I might give you a bonus."

"I'm much obliged. I can get him." Jones tried to sound reassuring.

"I don't want to see you again until the work is done. You hear me?"

"Yes. Yes, sir," replied Jones as he slinked away like the snake that he was.

The entrance to the ranch was decidedly nondescript. The wooden posts supporting the arch were in need of repair. Two of the letters spelling out the spread's name had fallen away and were gathering dust alongside the rutted trail leading into the place. I shook my head knowingly. The drought hadn't done Callahan any favors. This was my first clue as to the financial straits the man was apparently in. I headed up the trail, reckoning that it would take me to the house.

As I rounded a turn about a mile in, I saw the house laid out before me. It was clean and humble. For a man whose presence demanded that folks nearly bow to him back in Skidmore, this was no palace for a king. The place was deathly silent. I saw no livestock nor ranch hands. I hitched Tornado and strode up to the front door. I had just raised my fist to knock when the door swung open.

"Welcome to the KC Ranch. May I help you?" she asked as she batted her eyes provocatively.

"Howdy, ma'am. I'm Texas Ranger Lucas Dunn. Is King Callahan available?" I strove to remain professional as my eyes were drawn to her ample endowments as if by some magnetic force.

"Why, he's out at the barn. I'd be pleased to fetch him." She made a motion to move past me.

I couldn't miss the sweet smell of some fancy perfume and note the high quality of the dress she wore. It wouldn't have been afforded by most women in Texas. The ranch might have been struggling, but it was obvious that she wasn't. She was young. Wife? Daughter? I shook off her presence. I saw the barn off to my left. "Er, that's all right. I'm happy to go myself."

She locked on to me with a penetrating stare. "I'm sorry. I'm Mrs. Callahan. Do go right ahead, Mr. Texas Ranger." She stepped back into the house. "If y'all come back here, I'll fix some tea." She gave me one of those come-hither smiles some women could toss at a man. "Oh, and you can call me Irma." She gave me a little fingertip wave. Was there something about me that attracted this sort of behavior?

Tea? I thought. Coffee would be more like it. I tipped my hat and headed for the barn.

Callahan appeared in the doorway. He had just finished pulling up his pants and had bits of hay hanging from his shirt. His face appeared a bit flushed; not like the confident, commanding presence back at the restaurant. I saw something or someone move in the shadows behind him. "You looking for me?" he asked. There was that deep, sonorous voice I'd heard before.

"I'm Texas Rang…"

"I know who the hell you are," he interrupted. "What's your business here on my property?"

"Just looked to get acquainted, Mr. Callahan."

"Well, we're acquainted. Stick to yer knittin', boy. Now, git!" Callahan's face reddened a bit.

"Sorry, Mr. Callahan. I'll be departing," I said as I backed from the barn. "I'll be in Skidmore a while if..."

"Git!" he demanded.

The man had totally lost any composure. For the life of me, I couldn't figure why he was so all-fired nasty. I glanced around as I strode back toward Tornado. The barn was falling apart nearly as much as the rest of the ranch. Only a few flowerbeds around the house looked well-tended. That was likely from a woman's touch. Callahan was struggling. It occurred to me that he was easy pickings for someone to take advantage of. Men, especially those overly-prideful like Callahan, were easy marks for those with money and an outsized desire for power. I thought on how Callahan had appeared when I'd first entered the barn. It was pretty clear that he'd been engaged in some sort of sexual dalliance. The more I learned about the man, the more his life looked to be a mess.

As I approached Tornado, Mrs. Callahan gave me a little flirty wave. "Come back any time, you hear, Mr. Texas Ranger," she trilled.

I looked over my shoulder to see Callahan stalking in my direction from the barn. I didn't figure to get into any tangle, so mounted up, tipped my hat to Mrs. Callahan. Somebody was dangling cash under King Callahan's nose, and he was obviously desperate for enough money to salvage his ranch and keep his wife. Irma Callahan looked to be a handful.

So, Callahan wouldn't talk, Garcia was off doing his

sleuthing, the railroad spur was nearly completed, and Garth Jones was roaming about looking to kill me. If I couldn't rustle up something meaningful, Captain Hughes would be calling me to join the Frontier Battalion on the Rio Grande.

SIX
MONEY TALKS

WITH GARCIA HEADED who knew where and Jenkins pulling out after completing the spur, I was left pretty-much high and dry so far as viable leads. I decided to find Uriah Lott, the man who'd sold the SA&AP to the Southern Pacific. I saw a newspaper clipping that referred to the SA&AP as *Lott's Folly*. The man might be temporarily out of the game, but folks like him never languished long on the sidelines. It was even money that he was cooking up his next railroad venture. I reckoned I had nothing to lose.

If Lott wasn't the source of the money, he just might know who was. I tracked down Jenkins long enough to learn that Lott lived in Corpus Christi at present. Words had it that the man was close to Robert Kleberg, the man who'd married wealthy rancher Richard King's daughter Alice Gertrudis King. Of course, the nearby town of Alice was named for her. I'd tangled with a lawbreaker or two up that neck of the prairie. Alice was about a day's ride from Nuecestown. The town was founded as a railroad junction and shipping center for cattle. Lott's interest undoubtedly centered around Kleberg's ties to the railroads for shipping their cattle. For all I knew, Kleberg could be the money behind the entire scheme.

I saddled Tornado and boldly headed for Corpus. All in all, it was a tad better than a day and a half ride. I had plenty of time to mull over the case. I had the killer any time I cared to track him down and recapture him, but was determined to get to the money behind Garth Jones and King Callahan. Determined? Bull-headed? Yep. I was those things. On the down side, I sure hoped Jones wouldn't bushwhack me. Then again, I expect he'd given up trying the ambush tactic, as it had failed him twice. Jones wanted me mano-a-mano, face-to-face. I'm sure he became more determined every time he looked at his mangled hand. Ironically, I wanted to capture him, not kill him.

Corpus was a growing town. Its population had blossomed to roughly ten thousand residents, making it a thriving coastal city. The salt air from the Gulf of Mexico wafted in regularly, though occasional major storms were known to batter the bejabbers out of the city. My cousin Patrick Dunn raised longhorns on the northern seventy-five miles of Padre Island, the barrier that partly shielded the city when storms struck. Thinking on it dredged up memories of solving the vigilante case.

I reckoned that Sheriff McTiernan would be pleased to direct me to where I might find Uriah Lott, so I headed for the jail. I shook my head as I thought of his inept deputy who had allowed Jones to escape. McTiernan was undoubtedly embarrassed over that. He sure owed me favors.

McTiernan happened to be sitting on the boardwalk in front of the jail as I rode up.

"Howdy, Sheriff," I called out friendly enough.

McTiernan nodded. "Welcome, Junior. What brings you back to Corpus?" He took care to not mention Garth Jones.

"Looking to find Uriah Lott."

"Most days, you'll find him down at the city dock feeding the gulls," he responded.

"What do you know of him?" I asked.

McTiernan smiled. "Nice fella. Hurtin' for money. He's passionate about trains and gets caught up in railroad deals, but I see him more as a promoter than a financier. Expect that's why he's got money problems,"

This was enlightening. "Thanks kindly for the perspective, John. I'll check in with you after I find him." I smiled inwardly as I turned Tornado toward the city dock. If Lott wasn't the money behind the railroad mess, then who was? Perhaps, Lott would offer insight. Then again, in my experience, promoters tended to be full of blarney.

From McTiernan's description, I had a fair idea of what Lott looked like. He parted his hair down the middle, wore a bushy mustache, and sported a rather bulbous nose. That likely described a few men around Corpus Christi, but I sensed that there'd be a certain look of liveliness in his eyes that hinted at the entrepreneurial man within.

I reined in Tornado near the main dock and sat my saddle so as to have a decent view of the place. Hot as it was, there were several folks strolling about taking in the breeze wafting in from the gulf. The ever-present gulls flew around chattering and diving for food.

My patience paid off. A gentleman who roughly fit McTiernan's description ambled into view and began tossing pieces of bread to the gulls. The birds wasted no time flocking around the ready source of food. I dismounted and hitched Tornado to a nearby railing. I walked the hundred or so yards to where Lott stood, positioned myself about a dozen feet away, and stared out at the gulf.

"What you lookin' for, son?" asked Lott.

"Excuse me, sir?" I responded, as though surprised.

"I saw you watchin' me. Who are you?"

Lott was a perceptive fellow for sure. "I'm Texas Ranger Lucas Dunn, sir. I presume that I'm making the acquaintance of Mr. Uriah Lott."

"Well, you got that right. You've tracked me down," responded Lott with a smile and a twist of his mustache as he shooed the gulls away.

"Would you answer a few questions for me about railroads?" I asked.

"Any in particular, Ranger?" Lott asked.

"Have you heard of the killings up in Skidmore at the SA&AP spur project?" I began.

"Whew! It's sure hot today." He wiped his brow. "You get right to it, don't you, son?" responded the railroad entrepreneur. "Yes, I heard about them. Sad day for the railroads. Been trouble around those parts ever since the Southern Pacific took over the line. Yep, nothin' but trouble. That gol-darned Railroad Commission of Texas been no help at all."

"Do you have any thoughts on who might be behind the killings?"

"Don't have enough fingers to list them," replied Lott.

"Archer Parr influence?" I asked.

"Naah, he wouldn't mess in any violence. He's too savvy for that." Lott replied with a finger twist on his mustache.

Lott confirmed my own assessment of Parr. "You know anything of King Callahan?"

"Sonofabitch once you get to know him. Drought's been unkind. I expect he's desperate to keep that filly of a wife in fancy frocks." Lott chuckled. "Not sure he has the smarts to be leading anything, but he might do most anything for the almighty dollar."

"If Callahan or someone like him was involved, any idea who might be giving the orders?"

"Check out the Southern Pacific. I know it makes no sense, but skullduggery on their part wouldn't surprise me none." Lott chuckled again. "I like the way you're thinkin', son."

It seemed no love was lost between Lott and the commission. "Guess I need to wrangle a sit-down with King Callahan," I postulated.

Lott looked at me as though trying to put me together with something embedded deep in his memory. His eyes lit up in a sort of Eureka moment. "You wouldn't happen to be related to a Texas Ranger of similar name?"

"You'd be talking about my father, Luke Dunn. Yes, I'm his son." I was resigned to this sort of family tie-in. It would take some doing to ever hope to match the legendary exploits of my dad.

"Well, yer of good stock then," rejoined Lott. He tossed some bread to the gulls hovering overhead.

I gathered that meant that our conversation was over and started to turn away.

"I'm thinkin' on building another line south from St. Louis. Hope yer around in a couple years to keep an eye on the project." He winked and tossed some more bread.

"Thanks, Mr. Lott. I appreciate your advice." I tipped my hat, ducked a diving seagull, and headed for Tornado.

I felt as though I was back to square one. Somehow, I had to wrangle a meeting with King Callahan. I didn't feature enduring a repeat of the ranch incident. I sure as hell didn't want to be near Irma Callahan. She appeared to be pure, unadulterated trouble. Did I say *unadulterated*? I sensed adultery was very much in play with her. This case was ever more about following the money. Where there was big money, power invariably seemed to lurk.

I thought back on my dad's counsel that life isn't about where you are going but about whom you are becoming. Character was critically important to him. He would occasionally remind us that there are plenty of characters with no character. He recognized that character is not an inborn quality, it is developed through good life influences. As my dad found, it isn't always a comfortable process. He advised me that we often face situations that don't go our way, and it takes strength of character to endure them. So it was that I found myself dealing with the likes of Garth Jones and King Callahan. They couldn't in the remotest sense be considered men of character.

I needed to engage Callahan outside the bounds of his ranch at a place where it'd be tougher to dismiss me. Then, it hit me. I just might be able to corral him at Martha's restaurant in Skidmore. I mounted Tornado and off we rode.

SEVEN
TEMPTATION

THE PUNGENTLY SWEET aroma of perfume entered Martha's fine establishment well ahead of Irma Callahan. The woman sure was liberal in her application.

I sat near a window, casually sipping a fresh-brewed cup of coffee. There was one empty table between me and the one that was considered King Callahan's. The mixing of the aromas of coffee and perfume made for a decidedly foul mixture. Nevertheless, every head in the place turned at her entry.

She was hard to miss. In addition to her distinctive bouquet, she wore a purple satin dress with a corset beneath that thrust her ample chest into as full a view as church folk might endure. Her auburn locks were tied up in a bun that begged to be undone so as to free her locks to fall across the ivory luster of her nearly-bared shoulders. He lips? Whew! They were a luscious crimson that she parted ever-so-slightly, such that they begged to dance with the lips of another. Her dainty, white-stockinged feet were demurely slipped into black patent-leather shoes. She flicked a fan with graceful motions of her wrist as a sort of icing on her cake. Oh, and the diamond on her wedding ring was likely worth a king's ransom. Mrs. Callahan sat rather gracefully and accepted the coffee that Martha quickly delivered to her.

All of this begged the question of where her husband might be. Did King Callahan permit his wife to gallivant about alone? He seemed the jealous type.

I nearly choked on my next sip of coffee as Irma caught me watching her and offered a come-hither wink. I was saved for the moment by Martha placing a plate full of eggs, sausage, and biscuits before me. I didn't acknowledge Irma any further but took to eating. It didn't serve as nearly enough distraction for me. I kept thinking of Cassie and my boys, Sean and Bode. I'd come painfully close to yielding to temptation with that dangerous Diana Kilkenny witch back in Kerrville. Would tempting women become the lot of my solving of murders in Texas?

Irma sat there sipping her coffee and all-too-obviously ogling me. Could King Callahan be far behind? I hoped and prayed that he was.

What happened next shook me to the soles of my boots. Garth Jones slipped into Martha's restaurant through the back door and, with but a sneering glance my way, slid into the seat opposite Irma. While I had the feeling Jones would have fully rejoiced in the opportunity to shoot me dead, he wasn't about to start anything in front of Irma, much less the other patrons. Now, that begged the question of what Jones was doing here? Did King Callahan know or was this an illicit liaison?

I kept my eyes averted. Irma and Jones whispered briefly. Jones nodded ever-so-slightly as though acknowledging her message. She passed him a sealed envelope and placed a velvet sack atop it. The sack quite obviously contained a goodly cache of coins. Was it payment for some completed service or a down payment on a deed to be performed? The envelope was decidedly thick. Jones took the envelope and sack of coins, stood, and, with a taunting look at me, departed.

I finished my breakfast and was drinking the last few drops of coffee when none other than Arturo Garcia strode in. I nearly choked as he too took a seat opposite Irma. What was going on here?

The expression on Garcia's face when he saw me was akin to that of a dog caught with its nose in the treats box. He turned to Irma and gave her one of those looks that asks *what are you trying to do to me?* Garcia got up a tad angrily and hustled out with no further interaction with the temptress's wiles. Whatever was going on would have to wait.

The day was just beginning and had already been filled with more intrigue than anyone might see for months. What was going on here?

Irma was nonplussed. She watched Garcia exit and then turned to study me for a few seconds. Her bearing said that she was full of herself for her ability to control men. She sipped her coffee.

I began to sense that there was far more to Irma than her flirtatious carryings on. It also occurred to me that King Callahan might be in over his head. Money? Power? Sex? Control? The plot was on a high flame and in danger of boiling over.

Irma appeared to be about to say something to me when her husband strode in. King Callahan was well-dressed, hardly indicative of his apparent dire financial straits. He looked askance at me as he sat opposite her and nodded to

Martha who dutifully filled his coffee cup. Callahan looked from his wife to me and back, concluding that exercise with a look-what-I've-got sneer delivered in my direction. His celluloid collar did seem to curl a tad more from the heat radiating from his reddened neck.

I smiled toward the couple and motioned to Martha to refill my cup. I reckoned this little encounter just might get quite interesting. I saw Callahan fuming as Martha poured my coffee. I reckoned by this time that the more I irritated him, the better my chances of engaging the man. I preferred a level-headed conversation, but I'd be satisfied with most any communication at this point. Who was paying him to engage Garth Jones, and how deep was he in the morass of chicanery that was unfolding?

Irma placed her hand over his as though assuring her husband that she was the devoted wife. The irony of the moment in the wake of what I'd already witnessed was heavy. This was obviously a woman not to be trifled with. Little wonder that Uriah Lott stayed clear and the likes of Archie Parr would have nothing to do with this sort of game.

As I looked Callahan's way, I honestly had to admit that they made a very attractive couple, though in a diabolical sort of way. I lifted my cup and made a toasting motion toward them. Callahan's face grew just a tad redder while Irma offered her demurest smile. He was doing no favors to that collar of his. In a perverse sort of way, I was enjoying this little interplay.

Callahan finally had enough. He glared at Irma, then at me. He stood and pulled back his coat to reveal a .38 caliber Colt Army revolver that looked as though it itched to be pulled from its holster. "You stop that with my wife right now, Ranger! You hear me?" he growled.

I nearly choked on my coffee. He was calling me out. The remaining restaurant patrons scrambled out the front door with nary a look back. "You've got this wrong, Callahan," I advised. I was no quick-draw artist and wasn't sure how I might fare in a confrontation. This was no showdown in some dusty town street like certain storytellers depicted.

Callahan's face grew redder.

Martha paused at the kitchen door with a plate in each hand. "I've got y'all's breakfast here, Mr. Callahan." Strangely enough, she had the effect of defusing the moment.

"No harm intended, Mr. Callahan," I said as calmly as I could manage. "I'd just appreciate the opportunity to talk with you."

Irma placed her hand on his arm in a soothing manner. "Sit, sweetheart," she cooed. "It's okay."

Callahan slumped into the chair.

I don't know what was in his head, but the stress of it was surely driving the man to ruin. Did he know of Jones' and Garcia's visits? Or were they liaisons?

Martha placed their breakfasts before them. "More coffee?" she asked sweetly.

Callahan sighed and turned toward me. "What do you want to talk about?" he asked, as though yielding to my request might get me off his back.

"Railroads," was my simple reply.

Callahan looked about furtively, as though verifying that the restaurant was free of patrons. "Meet me at the livery down the street in an hour." He turned away and began eating.

I decided that a discreet departure was in order. "See you there, Mr. Callahan." I laid a dollar and a tip on the table, nodded gentlemanlike at Irma, and left the restaurant.

I waited beside the entrance to the stable. There was a cool breeze that brought much-needed relief to the sweltering heat that had taken over Skidmore. Nevertheless, I found myself swiping my neck with my bandana every now and then. I glanced at my pocket watch. Just about an hour had passed since encountering Callahan.

"He said an hour," came the voice. It wasn't King Callahan's.

"Irma?" I queried, hoping it wasn't her.

The aroma of perfume and warmth radiating from her presence was nearly overwhelming. "My husband won't be able to meet with you," she murmured, as she placed her hand on my arm. "May I help you?" She took my bandana and wiped my face. "I'm familiar with railroads," she added softly.

It had suddenly grown blazing hot.

"Let's get out of the sun," she urged. She grabbed my arm and pulled me with her.

I felt weak-kneed and unable to resist. I desperately needed to gather my wits. Was it the heat? The perfume?

"What was it that you wanted to know, Mr. Texas Ranger? How much my husband is being paid to stop the San Antonio and Aransas Pass line? Who is paying him?" She pushed me onto the hay in one of the stalls and stood over me. She lifted her dress, revealing more than I cared to see and drawing my eyes like a powerful magnet.

I nodded. "Y-y-you know who is paying him?" I stammered.

Irma kneeled. She seductively freed her breasts from her bodice and began unfastening my pants. "Bland Olson," she cooed. "Big money. In deep with the Southern Pacific."

I grabbed her hand before she could go further with her amorous endeavors.

Irma pouted. "You're such a big man," she pleaded. The air dripped with her sexuality. "I wanted to see if you're big everywhere."

"Where's your husband?"

"King? Why, he's dead," she said matter-of-factly.

My senses suddenly snapped back to reality. The intoxicating perfume, Irma's privates, her temptations mattered not. I intuitively knew that Garth Jones had delivered for her. She'd just admitted to a Texas Ranger that she'd had her husband murdered. Could I prove it? It'd be my word against what would surely be the sad pleas of a grieving widow. "Did you?"

She gave me her most provocative smile. "Have him murdered? Really, Mr. Texas Ranger. Why would a little old girl like me do such a thing to her loving husband?"

Damn, but she was a minx.

"Where can I find Bland Olson?" I persisted despite her wantonness.

She shrugged with disappointment. "Look to the rail-road commission. They ought to know."

I managed to break free of her grasping hands and stand. I was a tad shaky but determined to get on with my lawman duties. Making my way to Tornado, I focused on saddling up while being all too aware that she stood nearby, half naked. I reckoned to find my way to this Bland Olson person of interest, yet knew that I had to deal with my constant nemesis, Garth Jones.

I was about to mount up when Irma came up behind me and tried to relieve me of my revolver. I clamped my hand down hard on hers. I turned and nearly lifted her off the ground with my grip. Resisting the temptation to hit her, I gave her as tough a look as I could muster. "Never ever try that again." I pushed her back into the hay and mounted up.

"Don't leave," she pleaded. "Come back! Please!"

I struck a stone-cold visage as I rode away. I dared not look at her.

EIGHT
ANOTHER MURDER

WHERE ON GOD'S green earth was Garth Jones? Dare I try to capture him again? I'd threatened to kill him if ever I had to hunt him down again. Yet, Jones held information on and bore witness to essential elements of this case. I was concerned lest he find me first, though I took small comfort in recognizing that he was inclined to confront me rather than bushwhack me. Small solace indeed.

I was grateful for my escape from Irma's clutches. She was not to be trifled with. I pondered her connections. Arturo Garcia, Garth Jones, King Callahan, and now Bland Olson danced to her tune. Who else might I find within her web?

I pointed Tornado toward San Antonio, as the Railroad Commission of Texas had an office there. With Jones out there somewhere, I avoided the road leading toward the city and cut my own trail. Perhaps, I'd learn something of Bland Olson up in San Antonio, assuming I could reach him before he too fell victim to whomever was working to reshape the railroad landscape.

Jones ought to be sending me another of his notes. I

found myself sort of missing his not-so-veiled threats. I had reached Medic Creek as the sun dipped low on the horizon and decided to camp for the night. Other than the creek cutting through the mostly flat terrain, there were only grasses and low-lying shrubs with occasional live oak and mesquite sprinkled with cacti. A few pecan trees were reminiscent of the Nueces River to the south. While I had an eerie sort of feeling that someone lurked out yonder. There was no one in sight, and I had checked my backtrail. I felt safe in building a small cooking fire. Once the fire had gotten hot enough, I filled the small coffee pot with water and a liberal handful of grounds. To call it brewing was an exaggeration, but it made decent coffee.

What to eat? Not a problem. I waited a few minutes for deer to come drink at the creek. I just lay low with my Winchester in my lap. A deer would present a lot of meat for one man, but could serve me for a couple of days. What was left over would be enjoyed by the coyotes and buzzards. Not much went to waste on the Texas prairies.

A small doe dipped her head to drink. It was her last. A quick field dressing, some deft cutting, and I was fixed with venison for the next couple of days.

I built a simple spit over my campfire and roasted a venison steak. While it roasted, I cut thin strips to make jerky. It wouldn't be seasoned so well as Cassie would make it, but it would suffice for my ride to San Antonio.

I was busy preparing the venison strips and turning the spit when I heard a twig snap off, maybe a hundred yards away. Sound carried quite well in the evening silence of the prairie. It was easily distinguished from crickets, owls, frogs, and the like. My hands quickly grabbed my Winchester that had been lying close at hand.

"Wagh!" came the greeting.

I knew that voice. Buffalo Watts was out here roaming

the vast Texas prairie and had found me. "Get yourself in here, Buffalo!" I called out. My throwback to another era was still alive and kicking.

Watts came hobbling on in. His beard was a tad longer, and his sweaty buckskins were in need of repair, but he was getting on fine for a man who'd lost count of his years on this planet.

"You hungry?"

"Thusty, too," he said with an eye on my coffee pot.

"Have a seat," I said as I poured coffee into his tin cup.

He sat on his haunches and took a sip. "Damn, but yuh brew a nice cup of swill, Junior." He gave a chuckle. "Been followin' yuh all day. Yuh travel right quick, son."

"I'm headed to San Antonio. Captain Hughes has me working on some murders on the SA&AP."

Watts thoughtfully stirred the coals with a stick. "Do yuh know who done it?"

"Yes, but I want to find the money behind the killings."

Watts nodded. "Thet Garth Jones fella?"

I nodded.

"He been followin' yuh all day."

"Had a feeling," I replied. My intuition had been right.

Watts freed the roast from the spit, took a chew, and handed it to me. "Mighty fine eatin'," he noted with nary a hint of distraction. "I be thinkin' yer man is 'bout a hundred yards o'er yonder," he said, pointing to the east. "Idyut flushed an owl a bit ago."

I smiled. So, it was Jones who'd stepped on the twig, not Watts.

"How 'bout I mosey out thattaway," he whispered with a nod toward a live oak just beyond the circle of light cast by my campfire. "He surely be comin' in. While you talk at him, I git him from behind."

I nodded. "Reckon he's headed my way. Just heard another twig snap."

Watts silently eased himself to a position behind the live oak. He'd no sooner departed when Garth Jones strode in brimming with confidence. He finally had me where he wanted me, or thought he did.

"Care for some coffee?" I asked calmly.

My quiet calm sort of set Jones back a little. "I'll take all I want after I'm done with you."

"Did you enjoy Irma's charms?"

Again, he was a tad off guard. "You ain't sounding like a man about to die," he growled.

I took a bite of venison. "You wouldn't have a man die hungry, would you, Garth?"

In the firelight, I could see a dribble of sweat run down his cheek. Jones was befuddled by my attitude. "You want it standing or sitting, Dunn?"

"Shall I turn around, so you have your usual target?" I reckoned taunting him with the insulting reference to his cowardly habit of bushwhacking his victims would be enough distraction to enable Watts to sneak up behind him.

The surprised expression on Jones' face when he felt the muzzle of Watts' buffalo gun in the small of his back was priceless.

"Just place that rifle of yours real gentle-like on the ground, Garth. Do the same with your gunbelt." My Winchester was aimed dead-on at his chest.

Jones quite reluctantly obliged.

"Now, lie face down and hug that Texas dirt real tight."

Again, Jones complied.

While Watts kept his rifle aimed at Jones, I handcuffed his hands behind his back. With that accomplished, I helped him to his feet.

"Damn you, Dunn," he snarled.

"Seems me capturing you is getting to be a habit," I teased. "Maybe we can find a jail that you can't escape from."

"Ugly sonofabitch, ain't he," observed Watts.

"I had you dead to rights, Dunn. What's this old reprobate doing here?"

I laughed. "Buffalo Watts? Why he's whupped more Injuns and taken more beaver and buffalo hides than any ten people I know. If we'd have killed you, you'd be minus your scalp about now."

Jones was seething. The very fact that he'd failed once again at finishing me off had to weigh heavily on his ego.

"Was King Callahan your work, Garth?"

"Damn right," he snapped angrily. "Right between his damned eyes. Even cut off his privates." He laughed wickedly. "Reckoned to send it to Irma as a trophy."

"She pay you?" I attached a line through Jones' handcuffs and began wrapping the end around that nearby live oak.

"Money came from higher up. Damn whore wanted him killed, because he was running out of money and he wouldn't free her."

Once again, the story had taken an ugly turn. "Who?"

Jones stood tight-lipped as I finished tying him to the tree.

"He knows," said Watts. "Lemme persuade him." His knife shimmered in the light from the campfire.

Jones turned to me. "You wouldn't," he offered almost pleadingly.

"Just a little piece of hair...mebbe an ear," teased Watts. "I'll do it Lakota Sioux style."

Jones began to show signs of panic, as he trembled and tears welled up in his eyes.

I shook my head. "Last time I captured you, I told you that I'd kill you next time."

A diabolical smile stretched Jones' lips. "Can't do it, can you? You ain't no cold-blooded murderer." He was actually beginning to enjoy his predicament.

"Back off, Buffalo. We won't be cutting up his sorry ass." I found myself frustrated, as I'd have liked little more than to rid myself of Garth Jones. "I guess the nearest decent jail is in Beeville." I'd passed about ten miles to the east of the town earlier in the day, but it seemed the best choice in lieu of lugging Jones all the way to San Antonio.

"Shucks, Junior. Yer no fun at all," lamented Watts with a put-on wry grin.

"You'd have never taken me without your old friend, Dunn. And you don't have the guts to kill me." Jones laughed.

"That's enough!" I grabbed an extra bandana and tied it over Jones' mouth. Other than his muffled protests, I was done listening to him. I turned to Watts. "Come on, Buffalo. Let's finish dinner." I strode over to the campfire. The venison was now overcooked and barely edible. The jerky wasn't much better. "Damn, I'm calling it a night."

Watts looked at me. "Got a strange feelin', Junior."

"What's that mean?" I asked as I laid out my bedroll.

"Somethin' ain't right. I wouldn't be sleepin' in yer bedroll this night."

I shook my head. "Ain't right? That all you've got?" I continued to spread my bedroll.

"I ever give you bad advice, son?" said Watts in a fatherly tone.

I sighed and looked up to the sky. There was no moon, and, despite plenty of stars, visibility wasn't the best. I snuffed out the campfire, grabbed my saddlebags, and trudged off to the side of the campsite opposite and mostly out of sight of Jones.

"I think yuh got this in hand, Junior. I'll be moseyin'. Thanks fer the coffee an' grub."

This was just like Watts to leave after dropping a warning. I wasn't going to argue with him. He was ever his own man. I suppose it harkened back to his days hunting and trapping in the mountains. "Come back tomorrow and bury me," I said with a laugh and watched him disappear into the darkness. He was his own man, a loner through and through.

Jones looked up at me with one of those smart-ass looks in his eyes that made me want to bash his teeth in. He grumbled something unintelligible through the bandana as I made certain he was secured to the tree. Despite the dim light, I could see and smell that he'd answered nature's call in his pants. I reckoned there was a bit of justice to that.

"Sleep well. You'll need the rest," I advised. I gazed around into the darkness before easing on over toward the spot where Watts had advised, or rather warned, me to sleep. I shrugged upon passing my bedroll, all comfortable-looking as it lay. I nearly brushed a cactus as I sat down and stared up at the stars. I felt as though my progress on this case was a process of two steps forward and nearly two steps back. Jones certainly was no help. He'd effectively become dead weight. If I didn't kill him first, he'd get me or languish in the prison at Huntsville. At this point, the former alternative suited me just fine. The ground was hard and I yearned for my bedroll. Watts better have been right about *somethin' ain't right.*

I'm not sure what time it was. I'd finally and pretty much reluctantly fallen asleep when there was shouting and hoof-beats and horses whinnying. Bullets began buzzing around like bees, so I hugged the ground at my little hideaway. There was no point in becoming someone's target.

"Git on yer horse, dammit!" came a shout in the darkness. The sound of hooves circling was joined by several more shots in rapid succession. These were too close for my comfort, but I stayed put. "Come on! He be dead! Let's git oughta here!" someone yelled.

The sound of hooves trailed off into the darkness. Soon, it was replaced with utter quiet. Any wildlife had been stunned into silence. As the dust settled, I tentatively got up and cautiously walked to where the campfire had been. I could barely make out the live oak that I'd tethered Jones to. He was gone. "Damn!" I murmured. I turned to the spot where I'd spread my bedroll. My eyes just about popped from my head. Even in the starlight, I could see that it was riddled with bullet holes. Had I not listened to Watts, I'd be a dead man. I sat in the dust and tried to fully gather my wits.

There was no point in chasing Jones this night. Besides, he likely figured I was dead. Being dead could surely work to my advantage, as it had on the murders up on the Guadalupe River. I would need to get word to Cassie. Meanwhile, I needed to consider next steps. There was still that Bland Olson character to deal with.

I shrugged and lay back on my bedroll, as it seemed to be a safe spot now. Questions roiled through my mind. I wasn't worried about Jones for the present. I was curious as to who had raided my campsite and freed the lawbreaker? Who knew that I was headed to San Antonio? Why did they rescue Jones? Perhaps, he knew more than he was letting on. Whom might he give up to avoid languishing in jail or swinging from a noose?

Come morning, I'd head up the trail to Kenedy. There'd be no delays, as I didn't have to worry about checking my backtrail. I wondered whether my friend Buffalo Watts would be tailing me again.

I rode into Kenedy with no particular fanfare. Just eased along like most any cowboy passing through. As I recalled from my dad, the town site had been part of a royal Spanish land grant made back around the time of the American Revolution. The SA&AP put the community on the map back in 1886. It was originally named Kenedy Junction in honor of founder Miflin Kenedy, but shortened to Kenedy a year later. I'm not sure what made me think of its history other than it was a key junction for the SA&AP.

The first building I encountered was the barbershop. My hair was getting unruly and I sure needed the luxury of a shave. I hitched Tornado and went on in. The barber was finishing up with a customer, so I took a seat alongside a small side table. A copy of that day's newspaper, the *Advance*, was laid out with a headline that leaped out at me. "Damn!" I muttered under my breath. The headline read, *Deputy US Marshal Arturo Garcia Shot Dead*. I grabbed the newspaper and read about how they'd found his body and that of another man alongside the SA&AP tracks outside Kenedy. What were Garcia and whoever he was with doing here, and who killed them?

"You okay?" the barber asked.

I managed to settle myself. The haircut and shave would do me good toward easing my mind. "Yes, thanks."

He motioned me to the now-empty chair, so I placed the

newspaper back on the table and tried to relax in the barber's chair.

"I see you're wearin' a Texas Ranger badge." Barbers always seemed talkative, and this one was no exception.

"Yes," I responded with a minimum of words. I tried to get across that I wasn't in a chatty mood.

"Saw that headline, did yuh?" he persisted.

"Yes," I repeated my previous answer.

"Nasty business all them murders goin' on. It's like them dime-store novels."

I didn't respond, as he snipped at my hair.

"Funny how the latest killings be alongside them railroad tracks. Yuh think it has somethin' to do with the railroads?" The barber was anything if not persistent.

I kept my eyes closed and hoped he'd shut up.

"I guess yuh can't be talkin' 'bout a case, aye?" he said, as he lathered me up for a shave.

It was best not to talk when a razor is dancing across your face, so the shave was a welcome respite.

As he finished the shave and wiped my face with a warm, wet towel, he unloaded a final opinion. "Bet that railroad commission is tied up with it all," he said. "You know what they say 'bout power?"

I wondered how many others were of the same mind about the commission. Refreshed by the haircut and shave, I headed to the Railroad Hotel and its lunchroom, which was known as the Beanery for obvious reasons.

I had my choice of tables at the Beanery. A young lady quickly brought me a cup of coffee. Coffee was the very elixir of Texas. Her eyes riveted on my badge. "Texas Ranger! Did you hear?"

"Yes," I responded.

She seemed a tad flustered.

"What's good to eat?" I calmly asked.

"You been asked about," she said, concernedly.

Now, she had my attention. Who knew I was here and alive? "Who asked about me?"

"Don't know his name. He wore a black hat and shirt. One hand weren't any good." She'd just described Garth Jones.

How could Jones know I'd survived the escape only hours before and would be in Kenedy? Clearly, I'd underestimated Jones' treachery. The lowlife had apparently killed his rescuers and was dead set on getting me.

"You okay?" the young lady asked.

"Sure. Just give me a heaping plate of whatever," I paused. It was late morning. "Make it eggs, bacon, and fresh biscuits if you've got them."

"Beans on the side?"

I shook my head no, but had to smile at the bean connection. The little restaurant was aptly named. In any case, a good meal would afford me time to think. I thought I was free of Jones, yet he was apparently somewhere here in Kenedy. I reckoned I'd start with Sheriff Brack Morris

NINE
DESTINY

THE HAIRCUT, shave, and hearty breakfast served to put me in a great frame of mind. Plus, I figured that I didn't have to be concerned with folks thinking I was dead. I gave the server an extra tip and headed off to find Sheriff Morris.

I didn't just walk out the front door of the Railroad Hotel. I wasn't up to committing suicide. The young lady who'd served me breakfast directed me to a back door that opened onto an alley running alongside a building behind the hotel.

Where was Garth Jones? Was he still reckoning to confront me, or should I fear bushwhacking? I sensed that I wasn't going to be capturing him this time. I did lament that, as I still felt that he knew far more than he was letting on.

In my experience growing up with a legendary Texas Ranger father, gun duels in the streets of western frontier towns were mostly a manufactured concoction by writers with more interest in deadly drama than actual fact. The supposed professional gun-for-hire who could draw their gun the fastest and shoot an adversary with accuracy was pretty-much fiction. Ambush was the most common form of killing, though gunfights while robbing banks, stages, or trains, or even rustling livestock, could erupt in killings. Still, it wasn't the classic showdown on some dusty main street of a backwater town. I did recall hearing about the Earp brothers' gunfight on the streets of Tombstone, Arizona, about fifteen years ago. Bottom line, I didn't expect Jones to be so clumsy as to confront me in a gun battle.

I had a pretty-fair idea where the sheriff's office was, so I stuck to the alleys. Keeping a low profile was a must. I wasn't of a mind to make Cassie a widow, and I had a family to help raise. I emerged from an alley onto the main street. The sheriff's office was opposite me. I didn't feature walking across the street in broad daylight, but had little choice.

As fate would have it, a man emerged from the sheriff's office. A badge was pinned to his chest. I reckoned this was Sheriff Morris. I whistled, and he looked my way. I flashed my badge and motioned him to come to me.

He waved his hand for me to come to his office.

I could ill-afford this silly dance. I shook my head vehemently and motioned for him to join me.

Morris finally yielded to my insistence and walked across the street to me. "What's going on?" he asked as he drew near.

"I'm Texas Ranger Lucas Dunn of Captain Hughes' Frontier Battalion. I'm on a case to solve the recent railroad killings. The killer is here in Kenedy and looking for me."

"You the son of..." Morris began.

"Yes. But this killer named Garth Jones has already killed half a dozen men connected with the SA&AP Railroad. I've captured him three times, and he's managed to escape *through no fault of mine*. I emphasized that Jones' escapes were none of my doing.

"What do you expect me to do about this Jones fellow?" asked Morris.

"Where might a man on a murderous mission be likely to hang out here in Kenedy?"

Morris grinned. "I've heard of Jones. Slender fellow. Black hat and shirt. Sports a Colt and a Winchester. His style would be to wait for you beyond the Kenedy town limits and bushwhack you."

"He's got it in his craw to confront me. I already mangled his right hand with a bullet a few months back. He's got a score to settle with me."

"You been to the Railroad Hotel?"

"Had breakfast there a bit ago," I responded incredulously.

"He's been shacking with some fancy-dressed woman last I saw him."

"You didn't arrest him?" I asked. I had visions of Jones bedded down with Irma Callahan.

"No paper on him, Ranger Dunn. He hasn't broken any law here in Kenedy."

The sheriff was right so far as the strict interpretation of the law. No one had as yet put papers out connecting him with the railroad murders, much less what had gone before up in Kerrville. Part of that was my own fault for trying to capture him myself. I still didn't want him dead. "Look, Sheriff. I could use a little help here. Call it professional courtesy."

"I might," he replied.

"Would you be so kind as to determine whether he's in the hotel at present? I'm still hopeful of capturing Jones, and I'm sure your jail could use a resident."

Morris smiled. "I'll check it out." He took a couple of

steps toward the hotel and then paused. "What if he's not in the hotel?"

I shook my head. "You might consider watching my back."

Off he went.

Sheriff Morris returned about ten minutes later. He smiled as though he'd swallowed a canary. "Your man is in the hotel all right," he advised. From the creaking sound of the bed in his room, he's involved. Clerk said he's in room 308. And the woman is a looker."

"Much obliged, Sheriff." I reckoned to not waste any time and made a beeline for the Railroad Hotel.

When I arrived, the clerk was standing behind the desk with an anxious expression on his face. "I'm Texas Ranger Lucas Dunn here to capture an escaped felon." I flashed my Texas Ranger badge.

"There ain't gonna be gunplay?" he asked nervously.

"Don't know. Do you have an extra key to room 308?" I asked, trying to not sound hard-pressed for time. I had no idea whether Jones was a man of sexual prowess or of the wham-bam-thank-you-ma'am variety. Time was of the essence.

"Just got this here skeleton key. Opens all the rooms, sir," he replied. I thought he might soil himself right then and there.

"Is there any escape from that room other than the door?" I queried. I needed to get a feel for what I might be facing.

"There's one window, sir. It's a three-story drop clear to the street." The clerk was beginning to get excited as he began to feel involved.

I grabbed the skeleton key, drew my Smith & Wesson, and headed up the stairs. At the third-floor landing, I double-checked the loads in my gun before tip-toeing to the door at room 308.

I listened intently. The bed was creaking rhythmically, and there were plenty lustful noises of unbridled passion. I debated kicking in the door versus inserting the key. As the sounds of ardor seemed to be reaching a fever pitch, I inserted the key and unlocked the door. I swung it open. Jones and Irma were unaware of me at first. In fact, Garth was at the very height of his ecstasy when I announced myself. "Garth Jones, you're under arrest!" Can't say as I've ever seen a man turn impotent so suddenly. Irma screamed and covered her nakedness. Jones reached for his Colt hanging in its holster on the bedpost.

My shot went awry. I'd aimed for Jones' hand, but his lunge caused him to catch my bullet in his chest.

Jones' hand groped desperately for the gun, but couldn't reach it. He looked down at the bleeding hole in his chest and turned his ever-evil gaze toward me. "Damn, now you've gone and killed me." He lay back gentle-like on the down comforter.

Jones may have been near death, but Irma was very much alive. She drew a pocket pistol from under her pillow, cocking it as she swept her arm up to aim at me.

I didn't hesitate. My bullet carved through the flesh and bone of her shoulder, causing her pistol to go flying out of reach. "You don't move a damn muscle, madam," I ordered. "Or, I swear your next breath will be your last!"

"Y-y-you shot me!" declared Irma. "I'm a woman. How could you?"

"Get some clothes on, you damned whore," I replied. Yes, my words were ungentlemanly, but she was no lady deserving of respect.

Sheriff Morris appeared in the doorway behind me. "You okay, Dunn?"

I nodded. "Arrest her as an accessory to murder, Sheriff." I turned to Jones, who was struggling to breathe as blood soaked the bed linens beneath him and his face turned ever paler.

"Him too?" asked Morris.

"Don't think it'll be necessary, Sheriff." Jones was lying naked on his back with his legs splayed and his privates showing for all the world to see. I quickly threw a coverlet over him. "Get her some doctoring, if you'd be so kind."

"Jones! Don't you go dying on me just yet!" I said loud enough to wake the dead, which he almost was. "Who's behind this? Make right with your Maker, Garth Jones. Tell me now."

"Don't tell him nothing, you damned fool," screamed Irma.

Jones looked at me through rheumy eyes. His lips strove to form words, as blood gurgled from his mouth. "You better man," he managed. A half-smile creased his bloodied mouth. "B-blan…" That was all. He took his final breath.

Sheriff Morris was already half pushing and half-carrying a nearly-fainted Irma down the stairs. Somewhere in that process, she lost the dress she was trying to cover herself with. By the time she and the sheriff made it out of the hotel and into the street, she was buck naked. Blood oozed from her shoulder wound as he hustled her to the jail. "Somebody call Doc Peabody," he called, as he pushed her through the door to the jail. He threw her a blanket and locked the cell door behind her. "Doc's coming," he assured her. He couldn't help but leer just a bit at her exposed body. He was a man with a man's weaknesses for the flesh after all.

The clerk finally showed up at the hotel room. He gawked a few seconds. "Damn, yuh done it!" he announced.

"Go fetch the undertaker, son," I said as calmly as possible. I was already thinking about finding Bland Olson. I began gathering what I could of the belongings of the two recent room occupants. There was a leather bag filled with gold coins, perhaps a thousand dollars worth. No telling whether it belonged to Garth or Irma. It belonged to Karnes County now.

I hadn't wanted to kill Jones, but fate wasn't on his side. Now, I hoped some information might be squeezed from Irma Callahan. I say *squeeze* figuratively, of course. Was she mixed up in this or just a convenient pawn? I expected I'd soon find out.

With the clerk's help, the undertaker managed to haul Jones' body to his wagon and cart him up the street to an awaiting coffin. Kenedy had its own version of boot hill, and that's where the killer's body would be parked for eternity. They'd sell his horse to pay for the funeral. I felt that I sort of owed it to Garth Jones to show up at his interment. Interviewing Irma could wait. She wasn't in any shape to be talking just yet, anyhow.

A light rain cast a pall upon the burial proceedings. For what it was worth, given Jones' evil ways, I fashioned a crude cross. It was with a sort of justice that I hung his black hat on the cross. I felt pretty sure that his soul wouldn't be entering the pearly gates.

As I watched the final shovel full of dirt cover Jones' coffin, I thought of resuming my journey to see Bland

Olson. This entire case was a veritable snake nest of deceit and murder. I'd heard it said that power corrupts and absolute power corrupts absolutely. There was a head snake running this show, and it needed to be beheaded.

TEN

BREAK IN THE CASE

WITH JONES' funeral under my belt, it was time to have a chat with Irma Callahan. I was mulling over in my mind what it might take to get her to come clean about her involvement as I entered the sheriff's office.

Sheriff Morris sat in his chair with his spurs working at gradually carving notches in the top of the gnarly old desk that filled nearly half his office. "Howdy, Ranger Dunn," he greeted me.

"Mind if I have a chat with your prisoner?" I asked.

"Better make it quick. Some lawyer is bailing her out. Just waiting for the judge to sign the papers." He shook his head ruefully. "Ain't hardly just is it? I mean, you got the man who committed the murders, but some sonofabitch ordered those killings. I can tell you that Mrs. Callahan has been mum so far. Lawyer told her to stay quiet."

What else could go wrong with this case? "I'll give it a try, Sheriff."

Morris led me down a hallway to Irma's cell. We stopped. "I don't recommend you go inside, Ranger. She's likely to tear your eyeballs out," he said with a chuckle.

She sat fully clothed on the edge of the cot. Her shoulder was heavily bandaged and her arm in a sling. Otherwise, she seemed none the worse for wear. By her countenance, she looked ready to leave the jail. Irma looked up at me. "You...you sonofabitch! You shot me!"

"Looks like I didn't hit anything vital," I countered. "Sheriff says you're getting out of here."

"Lawyer says not to talk to no one." But for the sling, she'd have folded her arms in resentfulness. She did the next best thing and pouted.

She actually was a pretty woman, even without doing up her lips and eyes and dousing herself with perfume. She'd lost her bodice, so the naturalness of her curves was quite evident. She was attractive to men regardless of her wardrobe, and her posture reflected the confidence she stories in knowing what she could do with her body. I couldn't let her feminine wiles work on me. "What will Bland Olson tell me?" I ventured.

"Told you, Lawyer says I can't talk."

"You know you're going to do jail time. I can put in a good word for you to get you a lighter sentence." I likely would have no such influence, but she wouldn't know that.

"I surely would have enjoyed flipping the sheets with you, Ranger Dunn." She deftly avoided answering my question.

"Olson?" I repeated.

"He's wealthy. Big money."

I was getting a peek under the tent, so to speak. This Olson fellow was apparently involved. Was he the head snake? "Did you have your husband killed?" I figured to throw the question out there as a diversion. It might get her in the mood to answer more critical questions.

"The sheriff is back in his office and my lawyer will be at least another hour. You're a big man. Are you big all over?" she asked provocatively. "How about a quickie, Ranger Dunn?" Her wounded shoulder wasn't slowing her down.

I was glad the cell door was locked. "Is Bland Olson the head man, or is someone pulling his strings?" I persisted.

Irma sat back with a pout. She proceeded to lift her skirt to reveal her nether region. "You sure?" she asked with lips parted invitingly.

"Answer my question, Irma," I demanded. My patience was wearing thin.

Irma winked at me. "You tell Bland Olson that he has a small cock."

Perverse as it sounded, Irma had just revealed more than she'd likely intended. Railroads, murder, money, and now sex were all converging in a volatile mix. Would the relationship between Irma and Olson be the break in the case that I so earnestly sought?

I heard scuffling and voices from the office. Irma's lawyer was here sooner than expected.

"What the hell are you doing with my client?" snarled the lawyer, as he angrily led the sheriff down the hallway to Irma's cell.

Irma quickly covered her privates and stood in anticipation of leaving.

I gave the lawyer a silent once-over. "She didn't say anything, counselor," I said calmly. "I'm Texas Ranger Lucas Dunn of the Frontier Battalion. Mrs. Callahan was arrested for attempting to shoot me."

"I'm Len Dixon, her attorney," the lawyer declared and handed me his card. "You have no right to be questioning her."

"Just curious about someone she knows, Mr. Dixon. I meant no harm." I glanced at Sheriff Morris who simply stood there with a knowing smile pasted across his face. He'd obviously dealt with Dixon before.

Dixon turned to the sheriff. "You've got the papers, Sheriff. Unlock this cell."

I stood back to let Irma pass by and walk up the hall behind her lawyer. I wondered who was paying for his services?

Once Irma and her lawyer were gone, Morris sauntered on back to where I still stood beside Irma's cell. He looked at me, then glanced into the cell. "What's that?" he said, pointing to a slip of paper with something scribbled on it in blood. He stepped into the cell and picked it up. His eyes grew wide. "Damn!" he declared and handed it to me.

I read the note. "She says they're going to kill her?" I asked sort of rhetorically.

"We'd better follow her, Dunn," advised Morris. "She looks to be headed for a fall."

We both dashed out the front door of the jail and looked up and down the street. There was no sign of Irma or the lawyer. I shook my head. If her life was threatened, why had she gone with him when she could have stayed safely in jail? "I'll get my horse, Sheriff. They can't have gotten far." I saw my case, such as it was, unraveling before my very eyes. I desperately needed to corral Irma and definitely had to have a serious interview with Bland Olson. I reckoned this Len Dixon fellow was also involved in some way. I was learning that the more sophisticated power brokers employed lawyers and accountants. As the trail led to the top of any such operation, professionals were employed to find legal loopholes and even do a bit of finagling of the books.

With Garth Jones dead, I appreciated not having to worry so much about being eliminated. This case had sure evolved into a labyrinth of deceit and murder.

Sheriff Morris and I met down at the livery where we saddled up. The stableboy told us that a man and woman fitting the descriptions of Irma and her lawyer escort had headed toward San Antonio in a carriage.

It didn't require a whole lot of savvy to realize that our horses would overtake Dixon's carriage long before it reached San Antonio. How soon remained to be seen. I realized that unless we captured them in Karnes County, Sheriff Morris would part ways with me. Sheriffs tended to pay attention to a little thing called jurisdiction.

The road was wide, so we were able to ride two abreast.

"It looks to me like Mr. Dixon has company," I said to the sheriff, as I slowed to read the hoofprints of what appeared to be three horses. I expect he must be feeling right secure about now."

It was hard to tell under the broad brim of his hat, but I'd swear Morris' face had turned a shade whiter. "I can ride with you to a bit beyond the San Antonio River, Ranger Dunn." Morris was already setting the jurisdictional boundaries.

I could hardly blame him for looking to avoid a confrontation. Being outnumbered four to two was fraught with risk. When and if Morris left me, the odds would truly stack against me. Here I was going through all this to rescue a woman who most likely already told me all she knew. My hope was that getting her safely out of danger would loosen her tongue.

We rode hard through Karnes City. By hard, I mean a fast walk. There was no point in killing our horses. As we approached the northernmost outskirts, I was dismayed to come upon an abandoned carriage. "Damn it, Sheriff! They're all on horseback now." I dismounted and inspected the conveyance. It wasn't built for rough roads, so likely just as well that they'd cast it aside rather than risk a breakdown. There was an empty opened carry-on that had likely contained supplies for the trail. There were also a couple of empty boxes of ammunition. Assuming the escorts were armed, this likely meant that the lawyer was carrying.

This discovery sure enough changed the dynamic at play. We were now on equal footing transportation-wise, though Irma might slow them a little. Another few miles of more cautious riding, and the San Antonio River came into view. The border of Karnes County wasn't far beyond.

Morris and I pulled up. "They're not in sight, Sheriff. Can't say as I blame you for staying within your jurisdiction. Go ahead back to Kenedy, if that's your druthers." I had let him off the hook. There was no advantage to making the man feel guilty. We shook hands, and off he rode.

I rode Tornado across the shallowest crossing I could find and left the San Antonio River behind us. No sooner had I crossed into Wilson County than I saw trail dust being kicked up ahead of me. Morris and I had come so close yet so far. I'd soon be dealing with an armed lawyer, three hired guns, and Irma. I had no idea whether she'd be any help at all.

Setting her free of Dixon and the escorts looked to be a considerable problem. Intuitively, it made no sense to confront them directly. If the three escorts were hired guns, as I suspected, somebody might be killed, and I wasn't excited by the prospect of that somebody being me. They would have to stop sooner than later. They likely weren't anxious to be discovered, so I doubted they'd be stopping in Marcelina for accommodations appropriate to a woman.

If indeed they were planning her imminent demise, camping on the trail would work just fine.

I took a gander at the western sky. In an hour or so, the sun would be creeping behind the rolling hills on the horizon. They were pretty much tracing the San Antonio River, so wherever they spent the night would feature plenty of water and nearby cover.

I had closed to within a quarter mile. I already pegged them as not being especially trail savvy, as no one had bothered to check their back trail. As I watched them far ahead of me, I saw them veer off the trail toward some cypress trees near the river. There was high ground to my left overlooking the trees. I headed there figuring to surveil them with optimum effectiveness.

Upon finding a suitable spot, I dismounted. I hitched Big Red, grabbed my Winchester, and made my way about fifty yards down the hillside and ensconced myself behind a couple of trees where I could observe the goings on. Irma was seated on a blanket with Dixon guarding her, while the three hired guns made camp. They soon had a small fire going and were making coffee and cooking some concoction in a pot. It was likely a stew, though I was surprised they'd come up with anything nearly so ambitious. I was downwind, and that reduced the chance of them hearing me. I could hear snippets of their conversation, and it confirmed my suspicion that Irma was at grave risk.

Now, I had to figure out what to do. To that end, I wondered what my legendary lawman dad might have done? He'd surely have come up with a strategy. "Okay, Dad," I said to myself. "What's next?" On the other hand, my dad often had a companion like Three Toes or One Arrow to offer sage wisdom.

The ensuing darkness was lit by stars, a half-moon, and

a few fireflies. Harkening back to the skills Buffalo Watts taught us, I likely could have come within a dozen feet of the little band without being spotted. They had a pretty good fire going, and it was tough for anyone within the fire circle to adjust their eyes to someone standing in the surrounding ring of blackness. I'd heard stories of men attacked by wolves or mountain lions because they never saw the critters coming.

The five of them took their sweet time eating and bedding down. Two of the hired guns sauntered off to answer nature's call, and I heard them discuss having sex with Irma before delivering her for her reckoning in San Antonio. Dixon appeared to be the only thing between Irma and unchained passions. She wasn't helping the situation. She went down to the river under Dixon's guard to clean up. Raising her dress, and despite her bandaged shoulder, she answered nature's call with full display of her womanly assets. She dunked herself in the river. Upon emerging, her wet clothing clung to her, leaving nothing to the imagination.

I shook my head in dismay. If she kept up her temptations, I figured Dixon might be hard-pressed to hold back the hired guns much longer. They were already talking among themselves. I sat back behind the tree and watched the drama unfold before me.

"Yuh really fixin' to take thet bitch to San Antone, Mistah Dixon?" asked the largest and gnarliest-looking of the escorts. "She sure looks like she could use my pecker." A deep scar ran down the right side of his face, and part of an ear was missing. They combined to give him an evil appearance. His bulging muscles threatened to burst from his shirt. He gave the impression that what he lacked in brains was compensated for in muscle and vileness.

Dixon's hand held a Colt Peacemaker. He didn't seem to

be taking any chances. "Y'all just settle down. Orders are to take her to San Antonio. She is to arrive unharmed."

"She ain't no virgin. What's it matter?" piped up one of the other escorts with a near-toothless grin. He grabbed his crotch and swiveled his hips as though humping a woman. "Come on. Let us have a piece. Who's to know?"

"You are being paid to ensure Mrs. Callahan's safety. Settle down. We'll be leaving early."

I picked up just a hint of a tremble in Dixon's voice. Could he stop the three escorts if they decided to have their way with Irma? I had no idea how effective the man was with a firearm. He sat close to Irma. I didn't get the impression that he could stop an attack even with his hand on his revolver.

Irma didn't seem to mind. She was looking for an escape. Setting the three hired guns against Dixon appeared to be aimed at eliminating enough of them to enable her escape.

I heard a noise behind me. Big Red was picketed too far off for him to have made the sound. I gently slipped my Smith & Wesson from its holster and prepared to turn. There was a rush, and suddenly Buffalo Watts was sitting beside me. "Damn," I whispered. "You nearly got yourself killed."

Watts delivered one of his all-knowing smiles. "But I'm alive," he whispered. "You enjoyin' the show?"

I nodded. "Waiting for the curtain to go up."

Irma lay back on her bedroll with her dress hiked up well above her knees. She winked and pouted her lips provocatively at the escorts.

It was too much. "Seth, I've got this heah lawyer covered. You get firsties." The man had his gun aimed at Dixon.

Seth was the big man who'd first suggested sex with

Irma. With anticipatory slobber running down his chin, he began to drop his pants as he made his first step toward Irma.

Two explosions tore the air apart. Seth stopped in his tracks. Letting go of his grip on his pants, he stared down at a bloody hole in the center of his chest. He gave an incredulous look toward Dixon, who was already pitching forward with a bullet through one eye.

Irma momentarily appeared stunned but quickly gathered her wits and managed to grab Dixon's gun. The bandaged shoulder slowed her down. She was too late. The man who'd shot the lawyer was on top of her.

The third hired gun moved toward them. "Screw her, Slick. Show thet bitch yer a man!" he hollered.

Slick was squirming on top of Irma while wrestling to lower his pants.

Underneath, Irma was desperately trying to get the muzzle of Dixon's gun pointed into Slick's body.

The gun was tangled in her own dress that Slick had hiked up nearly to her shoulders.

I had seen enough. I winked at Watts. "Curtain time," I said. I raised the Winchester into firing position, chambered a round, and took aim at Slick's butt. The bullet plowed through Slick's rhythmically humping butt just about the time he heard the report.

There's nothing like a bullet to bring a man's passions to a halt. Slick yowled and drew back from Irma. The third escort looked in my direction and drew his gun.

"If y'all want to meet your Maker, try it!" I warned.

Watts sat beside me, chuckling. "Damn good show, Junior. Helluva curtain call."

I moved from my hiding place and began walking toward the campsite with my Winchester at the ready.

Slick was groveling on the ground with his now-bloody

hand gripping his bare butt. "Yuh shot me, dammit!" he said, eyeing his remaining companion.

"Twern't me, Slick," the man said with a nod to me and Watts emerging from among the trees.

Slick finally saw me.

"Drop your guns. I'm Texas Ranger Lucas Dunn, and y'all are under arrest."

Meanwhile, Irma had gotten up and begun to slink off toward the horses.

"And you, stay away from those horses," I called to her.

Watts deftly moved between her and the cayuses just to be sure.

Irma's shoulder sagged. There was no escape.

Slick was still lying on the ground. His wounded butt wouldn't permit him to sit. "What are yuh gonna do with us?" he groaned.

I looked down at the two bodies still bleeding out and shook my head. "They've got a jail up ahead in Floresville. I reckon I can park you two there, and Slick here can get a doc to look at his butt."

Irma had quickly gotten herself back together. "What about me, Mr. Ranger?" she cooed and made sure I couldn't miss her cleavage.

I exchanged a knowing look with Watts. The grizzled former mountain man shook his head. "Good luck with this one, Junior," he said with a wink.

Irma turned to Watts at the sound of his gravelly voice. "Looking for some fun, old-timer," she said with her voice oozing lust. She was desperate and sure didn't know the likes of Buffalo Watts.

"Why ma'am, if I could avoid a heart attack giving you my all, you'd be tempting me. But it's not your day." He turned to me. "You need her tied, Junior?"

Irma's shoulders sagged. She'd been saved from a

deadly end, but was now my prisoner. She was, at the least, an accessory to multiple murders.

I secured the two remaining escorts and Irma to a cypress and slept the night while ignoring Slick's moaning and his fellow escort's gross snoring. Watts spent the night. To his credit, he fixed coffee at sunrise. I was in a bit of a fix. Watts, ever his own man, took a final sort of wistful look at Irma and then departed. At least, he'd helped me get the baggage loaded up. Seth and Dixon were blanket-wrapped and draped over saddles. We arranged for Slick to ride side-saddle to take pressure from his rear end, and the third hired gun was tied to his saddle with hands tied behind him. Irma? I had to tie her shoulder strap up such that she had to stop untying it to reveal a breast. I tied her ankles to the saddle fenders. She kept yakking, so I tied a bandana over her mouth to keep her quiet. Our caravan surely made for quite a sight as we headed for Floresville.

We only passed two travelers on the journey northward. I'd displayed my Texas Ranger badge, so while strange looks were elicited, no one raised any questions.

I disposed of all but Irma in Floresville and rode on toward San Antonio with her. Every time I glanced back at her on the trail, she had a pleading look in her eyes.

We were about five miles shy of San Antonio when I reined us in to take a rest before heading into the city to find Bland Olson. I untied Irma's legs from the saddle fenders, trying my best to not touch her. Easing her from the saddle, I was forced to grab her by the waist. As I brought her to earth, she leaned into me and explored my crotch with her free hand. The woman simply would not give up.

"Please," she pleaded. "Please don't take me to San Antonio. I'll do anything you want."

I sat her on the ground under the shade of a cypress.

With her sexual wiles not working on me, I could see in her eyes that she was working up another approach. "I need to pee," she said.

"Fine. Go ahead," I replied.

"Well, don't look." She gave me her attempt at an innocent holier-than-thou expression.

"Irma Callahan, I've already seen how you play that game. Go ahead and pee, but I'm not letting you out of my sight."

She pouted, leaned back against the tree, lifted her dress, and gave me a defiant look as she relieved herself. Finished, she walked over to a nearby cypress and sat while I watered our horses.

"It'd go easier for you if you'd tell me what this Bland Olson's involvement is and how you found yourself in this nest of rattlesnakes." I was earnestly trying to get her to come clean.

"If I tell you, they'll know. They'll kill me." She took a crestfallen pose.

"Well, if what you feared is true, they apparently have already decided to eliminate you. You might have a better chance by telling the truth. I might be able to help you get away." I wasn't certain I could deliver on protecting her, but I did figure to try.

"I can't talk with you standing there looking down on me." She stared out beyond the river.

I grabbed a log, dragged it over in front of her, and sat. "Okay. What do you know about this affair?" I spoke as calmly as I could. Despite her disheveled condition, she was still quite fetching to the eyes.

She sighed. "Not much. I know that it involves the

Southern Pacific looking to destroy the SA&AP. This Bland Olson is tied to the Railroad Commission of Texas, but he's no friend of the commission. He's tied to the Southern Pacific owners, and there's some to do over the SP not being legally able to own the SA&AP. I don't know how that works."

"How did you get involved?" I asked.

"Olson visited Skidmore," she replied.

"And?" I pressed.

"Come on, Ranger Dunn. You know how I am." She looked dead-on at me. She sighed. "We were lying in bed, and he intimated to me he might be looking for help driving the SA&AP out of business. I mentioned that the drought had brought us hard times. Olson said he'd be willing to pay for help."

"Did you know this included murder?"

"Not at first," she answered regretfully. "That Garth Jones brought that to the mix. Then that deceitful Deputy US Marshal got involved."

I nodded at her mention of Arturo Garcia. He had me duped, too. The rest of her story was easy enough to figure out. She found herself in the game too deeply and unable to get out. "Now, they want you gone, because you know too much."

"Ranger," she pleaded. "They killed my husband."

"And at least a half dozen more by my count," I reminded her. I pondered how best to get her to a safe place. I had family who might shelter her, but she wasn't exactly the pinnacle of morality. She'd brought whoredom to a level transcending houses of ill repute. But for the distance, I'd escort her to Heaven's Gate and put her under my ma's wing. Even Cassie might look after her. I shook my head. What was I saying? I knew nothing of Irma's past.

Where was she from? Who was she before marrying King Callahan?

"Where will I go?" she lamented.

I had some vague familiarity with hotels in San Antonio. My cousin Nick Dunn had stayed at the Menger Hotel near the Alamo. I decided to make that our destination. Getting there would be easy enough, keeping Irma safe, not so easy. I reckoned I would put her up under an assumed name for a couple of days while I sought Bland Olson. I wasn't convinced that she was fearful enough to stay hidden, so I was resigned to manacling her to a bedpost or other solid mooring. But first things first. We remounted and set off for San Antonio.

ELEVEN
SHOOTING BLANKS

SAN ANTONIO WAS a bustling city of nearly fifty thousand folks. Being used to small Texas towns and vast expanses of prairie, the contrast was striking. Despite my size and being accompanied by a still quite disheveled woman, we blended right in with the masses of people on the streets. I asked directions a couple of times before finding the Menger Hotel.

We finally rode up to the main hotel entrance. The building was imposing, to say the least. It rose up three stories and featured wrought iron balconies across its front. What looked to be around a dozen lamps stood out front, ready to light the area for guests at night. The wagon ruts in the dirt streets seemed a bit anachronistic before so fancy an edifice. Surreys and carriages were parked on the plaza across from the hotel, and a seemingly endless parade of men on horseback rode by.

I had untied Irma's legs from the saddle fenders just as we entered the outskirts of the city, so she wouldn't look like a prisoner. I hitched both horses and helped Irma down. She winced as the horse bumped her wounded shoulder. She then made eye contact with me, such that I quickly released my hold on her waist. Would she never give up her flirtatious ways?

I grabbed my saddlebags and we headed for the front desk. We waited while the clerk helped another customer. Finally, the clerk—Ramon by his nametag—was clear, and I strode up with Irma in tow.

Ramon gave us a disapproving once-over.

I sighed and displayed my Texas Ranger badge.

"How may the Menger Hotel be of service?" asked Ramon patronizingly.

I already reckoned that I'd eventually have a chat with Ramon's manager. "We need a room."

He looked sneeringly at Irma.

I'd had enough. I leaned over the desk. "I'm Texas Ranger Lucas Dunn of Captain John Hughes' Frontier Battalion. I'm on a special mission. This woman is my prisoner and must be kept with me. If you don't cooperate, I will arrest you for obstructing justice." This was partly hooey, but the clerk didn't know that. A touch of fear crept into his expression.

"Yes, sir, Ranger Dunn." He had me sign the register and gave me the key. "That will be room 208."

"I'll take both keys and the master." I wasn't chancing the possibility that this whipper-snapper of a clerk might tip someone to my prisoner's presence.

"We can't give out the…"

"Just be for tonight," I assured him.

He handed over two room keys and two master keys. "This is all of them?"

He nodded.

"I have two horses hitched out front. See to them." I turned, then paused. "And send a hot bath to the room for the woman." I was careful not to call her a lady, as I thought that dishonored the natural order of things. I picked up my saddlebags and Winchester, grabbed Irma, and headed for the stairs to the second floor. I stopped and scanned the grand foyer to be sure no obvious trouble lurked. No one appeared suspicious.

I urged Irma on ahead of me. I made one final scan of the foyer. A swarthy-looking man on the far side looked a tad suspect. He caught me looking at him and darted out the front door. Irma had paused, so I nudged her along.

We soon were standing before room 208. I turned and crossed the hall to room 207. Using the master key, I let us in.

"I thought we were to be in room 208," said Irma with concern.

"Trust me," I responded.

I closed the door behind us.

"What now?" asked Irma.

"Just wait, and no matter what happens, stay quiet."

Sure enough, a mere five minutes later, there was a crashing sound from across the hall followed by gunfire. Cold silence followed as the attackers realized they'd been duped. They turned the air blue with cussing as they stomped away down the hall. The last thing I heard was somebody grumble that they intended to talk with Ramon.

Well, it didn't appear that the famed Menger Hotel was a safe place for Irma, not to mention me. I didn't take kindly to folks shooting up a room I intended to occupy. I peeked out the door from room 207 and saw an exit at the far end of the hall.

"Where are you taking me?" cried Irma.

"Stay quiet. There's another hotel. It's not far." I'd heard of the Emma Hotel and reckoned it might be our only chance at finding some momentary respite. It seemed that we had walked straight into the rattlesnake nest.

We exited the rear of the Menger. No one was in sight, though I was sure folks were out looking for us. I figured to worry about the horses later as I led the way to the Emma.

"Where can I find Bland Olson?" I asked the desk clerk at the Emma Hotel after registering. This time, I used an assumed name, showed no badge, and hinted to the clerk that I needed a quiet room to pleasure the woman I was with.

He shot back an incredulous look, as though everyone ought to know where to find the man. "Up thataway," he replied, pointing up the street from the hotel. "Office is under the Railroad Commission offices."

I'm sure my dallying with a woman, plus looking to meet Bland Olson, seemed like a contradiction of intentions to the clerk. "Thanks kindly. If anyone inquires about a man and woman looking like us, you be sure to tell them you haven't seen any such folks." I gave him a steely-eyed look. "If there's a problem…" I gestured with my finger to my head and my hand forming a gun. I left a couple of silver coins on the clerk's desk and headed to our room.

Once in the room, I pulled the manacles from my saddlebag and slipped one of the cuffs around Irma's right wrist and the other to the post of the steel-frame bed. She was going nowhere.

"Must you, Ranger Dunn?" she half-pleaded. Memory of the sound of gunshots back at the Menger was surely still ringing about in her head.

"You'll be safe. I won't be long." I tried to sound reassuring.

She pouted and sat on the bed.

I checked the loads in my Smith & Wesson and headed

out to visit Olson. I hoped that he'd actually be in his office. With what I surmised to be his men hunting for me, he'd surely be at his home nest awaiting news of my demise.

While it was still broad daylight, there were enough shadows cast by buildings that I was able to move as unobtrusively as could be expected. In but minutes, I found myself pushing through the doors to the building and reading the tenant directory. Olson's office was directly up the hallway before me. I stood in front of the door to his office for a moment to gather my wits. Hopefully, I was on the cusp of resolving what I'd begun to think of as the case of the railroad murders. Yes, I recognized that it reached beyond murder.

I didn't knock. The door was unlocked, so I pushed on through. A man sat at a reception desk in the outer office, mouth open and a bullet hole between his eyes. Resigned to what I expected to find in Olson's office, I barged ahead with my gun drawn. His chair was toppled over and the body fit the description I'd been given of Bland Olson. He'd been shot at least three times that I could see, and blood was everywhere. My shoulder reflexively slumped with disappointment. What was going on here?

I looked around the office. A drawer containing a pocket pistol was opened, but Olson hadn't had a chance to use it. File drawers were open and had obviously been rifled through. What were they searching for, and had they found it? I scanned the office looking for some clue of a place where valuables might be hidden.

I was about ready to give up. My investigation was shooting blanks so far. I was about to leave the office empty-handed when I chanced to glance at the floor under

Olson's desk. There was an odd misalignment of the wooden floorboards. I pushed the desk aside to reveal a hidden compartment. Using my Bowie knife as a lever, I managed to pry the boards loose. A small vault was revealed. "Damn!" I muttered.

If someone went to this much trouble, there had to be something incriminating in the vault. I wrestled it free of its moorings and sat it on the desk. Of course, it was locked, and there was no way I had the means or time to open it in Olson's office. I'd been fortunate thus far that no one was around. If the law were to arrive, I'd have some serious explaining to do, plus I would most likely lose the vault. I judged that it weighed about twenty pounds. Ducking it under my arm as best I could, I headed back to the Emma Hotel.

My luck was holding. Irma was still manacled to the bed. "We need to get out of San Antonio quickly," I told her.

Her eyes couldn't miss the vault that I'd placed on the table near the bed. "What's that, and why are we leaving?"

"Olson is dead."

With a gaping jaw, she emitted a sharp gasp. "No!" she exclaimed.

"I found this vault in a hidden compartment under his desk. We need to get it open, but doing it here will make enough noise to awaken the dead."

She pulled herself together and looked at me knowingly. "I may be able to open it." She pulled a pin from her hair. "Let me loose from these things."

I unlocked the manacles. "You'll need to hurry."

Irma went to work trying to pick the vault's lock.

I watched her work. I had to admit that she wasn't bad

to watch. She was as fetching as she was industrious in her work.

After about thirty minutes of digging and twisting the hairpin in the lock, she sat back and swung open the door to the vault.

I stood and peered inside and felt a brief wave of disappointment. A single envelope lay within the vault. "This better be good," I said upon pulling it out. I broke the seal and opened the envelope. The masthead on the letterhead branded it as *bona fide* stationery of the Railroad Commission of Texas. Unfolding the official-looking document, I began reading. "This is damning," I said.

"What do you mean?" she asked as she tried to read the letter over my shoulder. Her closeness was too much.

I pushed her off, folded the letter, and stuffed it in my pocket. "We've got to leave."

"But...why?" she persisted.

I stopped and laid as steely-eyed a gaze as I could muster upon her. "If you knew, they'd have an even greater reason to kill you." I headed for the door, dragging Irma behind me. I needed to retrieve our horses from the stable near the Menger Hotel. That might very well be a challenge. I was confident that I was on the cusp of solving the case.

We crept in the shadows along a wall behind the Menger. I had to give Irma credit for keeping up with me. After all, I was her only hope for safety. With the stable in sight, we had to cross an open expanse of roughly ten yards. We'd be exposed but had little choice.

"Can I have a gun?" she whispered.

I looked at her as though she were crazy. "Just stay close," I advised. I scanned the area. Seeing no one, I prepared to dash across the exposed area. "Let's go!" I commanded.

We dashed across to the stable. Halfway, Irma tripped. I wound up mostly dragging her. We stood breathing heavily in the shade of the stable entrance. So far, so good. I adjusted my eyes to the dim light.

I saddled Tornado and a second horse for Irma. I was confident in how Tornado would perform, so I selected what I judged to be a fine piece of horseflesh for Irma. She'd need to keep up with me.

"Why are you doing this?" she asked. "Why are you concerned about me?"

I really had no answer save for the morality of protecting another human being. Given her carryings on, it sure wasn't a matter of chivalry. "Don't figure to let you die," I answered.

We mounted up. Now, we had to escape unscathed from San Antonio. "We're going to ride hard. You ready?" Not knowing who our enemies were, it would be akin to riding through a gauntlet with possible danger on all sides. "Let's go!" Off we went.

The Menger Hotel and San Antonio were soon left in our dust. If anyone was gunning for us, they hadn't shown up to our party. I turned our horses northwest toward New Braunfels.

"Why this way?" she hollered, as she galloped alongside.

"Got friends there," I shouted back.

A little better than a mile outside of San Antonio, we pulled up near Cibolo Creek. The horses desperately needed a blow after such a hard ride.

TWELVE
BUSHWHACKER

WE SAT in the shade of a live oak while the horses slaked their thirst. Irma eased over to the edge of the creek and splashed herself with water, partly to wash off trail dust, partly to cool off, and partly to tempt me with her womanly charms. There was certainly nothing fancy about her at this point in our journey. Her clothes were decidedly shabby, and a bit too much of her was exposed as a consequence. Irma was excess baggage in the sense of slowing me down. She needed protection, but was in this predicament of her own making. I had a feeling that she'd led a rather sordid past before marrying King Callahan, but she wasn't inclined to reveal anything of it.

She knew I was watching her at the creek side. What man wouldn't? "Could you replace this bandage?" she asked with an almost come-hither tone. "It's gotten dirty, and I fear infection."

It was a legitimate concern. "I'll see what I can do," I responded reluctantly. I knew that I had some bandages in my saddlebag.

Irma promptly released the shoulder ties to her dress. The top dropped to reveal her breasts.

This wasn't what I needed, but I'd do my best to ignore her overt attempt at temptation. I took out my Bowie knife and began to cut away the bandage from her shoulder. The wound was still a nasty one, and all the activity of the past few days had not contributed to its healing. I cleaned it with creek water as best I could and rebandaged it.

"I like the feel of your hands," she cooed. "Your hands are rough but gentle." She gave me a provocative look and pursed her lips as though kissing. Her disheveled hair and streaks of dirt on her cheeks actually made her incredible desirable.

I retied the shoulder ties of her dress, relieved at covering her breasts. My manhood had reflexively risen to the occasion, but, blessedly, her back was to me.

"Is that all, Ranger Dunn?" she murmured and thrust her chest out so far as her bandages would permit. Did this woman ever think of anything else?

"Afraid so, Irma," I said, shaking my head. "We must ride," I added as coldly as I could muster.

I helped her into her saddle. No sooner had I turned my back than she put her heels into her horse's sides and bolted. I stood there and watched. I no longer had it in me to protect the ungrateful woman, much less waste mine and Tornado's energy chasing her. I sighed, climbed into my saddle, and pointed my horse toward Austin. I bet I hadn't managed to travel a hundred yards when I heard the crack of a rifle split the air. "Damn," I muttered.

I gave myself credit for not being foolhardy and charging in the direction of the gunshot. I had a feeling someone had caught up with Irma. That meant that we'd been watched for some time. Whoever it was had been waiting for a clean opportunity to bushwhack Irma. Was there anyone remaining who was involved in this railroad rattler nest? I patted the letter stuffed in my shirt pocket. The man named in it would be my last hope.

Meanwhile, what to do about Irma? Do I leave her to rot in the Texas sun? Where was the bushwhacker, and might he be after me? She couldn't have gotten all that far. Resignedly, I headed Tornado in the direction she headed.

As I drew near, I saw her horse still galloping off across the distant prairie. Then, I heard the creaking leathery noise of a horse's tack and a whinny. Someone was on the scene. There hadn't even been time for buzzards or coyotes, but another scavenger was apparently at work. I slid from my saddle, grabbed my Winchester, and eased up a rise that, as it turned out, overlooked the scene of the crime. There was a man rifling through what few belongings Irma had. What could he be looking for? He was so focused on the task at hand that he had no idea I was watching him. If he had indeed followed us, he must have known that I would still be around. Could he really be that careless?

I felt something hit my head. I guess it knocked me out cold pretty much instantly.

Groggy as hell. My head hurt. My hands were sticky, and I discovered it was blood. Mine. My eyes focused on dirt. I tried to rise. Nope. I tried again. I managed to roll over. I was lying under a starlit sky. Oh, but my head ached something fierce. I felt around me. My holster was empty. From my limited field of vision, I was unable to see my Winchester. I heard a yip and looked down toward my feet.

A coyote was staring hungrily at me. "Sorry, Fido," I thought. "I'm not dinner just yet." It wasn't too tough to figure out that I'd been shot. Blessedly, it hadn't been enough to kill me. I could feel my Bowie knife still in its scabbard on my hip. It was now the only weapon I had.

I patted my shirt pocket. The letter was gone. Struggling, I propped myself up on my elbows. This was progress. Now, I needed water and a bandage. I looked about for Tornado. I tried to whistle, but my lips were too dry. "Tornado," I called as best I could. My voice cracked terribly.

Thanks be to God, whoever had bushwhacked me had been unable to corral Tornado. "Come," I hand-signaled him. He eased over near me, though I suspected he smelled the blood as he trembled a bit. "Tornado. Lie down," I told him. We'd done this before, but not for some time, and I was usually standing beside him. Thankfully, he remembered and dropped to the ground beside me. I tried to grasp the saddle horn but couldn't quite touch it. My head swam a bit. I patted Tornado's flank. "Easy, boy, I muttered. I mustered myself as best I could and reached for the saddle horn again. Got it! A little more effort, and I had pulled myself up to where I could raise my leg across the saddle. Now, I was in an awkward fix. I rested a moment. Tornado was being ever so patient. Determined to sit in the saddle, I pulled myself into a sitting position atop the wonderful contraption. "Tornado. Up," I ordered. With but a light whinny, he stood. I nearly fell from the saddle, as my head swam. I thought I might faint. I'd lost plenty of blood, the ground bore evidence of that.

From my vantage point atop Tornado, I scanned the area. The sun was low on the horizon, so hours had passed. Buzzards and coyotes had been disposing of Irma's remains. What they didn't devour, the flies enjoyed. I'd sure hoped for a better end for her; maybe even salvaging her life. Yet, somehow, there was justice, given her devious ways and connection to this nest of vipers I was pursuing.

There had apparently been at least two bushwhackers, as one had shot me while I was surveilling the other. Dang, but that had been careless of me. I should have known better. I urged Tornado toward the creek. I desperately craved water and needed to clean and bandage my head.

We found the sheltered spot beside the creek where we'd rested. Tornado, bless his heart, repeated his trick and sank to the ground. I eased out of the saddle, grabbed the last remaining bandages from my saddlebag, and crawled to the creek. My reflection in the water revealed an ugly bullet crease. It hurt like hell, but I cleaned it as best I could. The pain nearly knocked me out, but I gritted my way through. Once bandaged, I sat back against a tree to rest from the exertion and to think.

Was I on a wild goose chase? I'd found the killer of the railroad workers. Technically, I'd solved the case to which I'd been assigned. I cogitated on my situation. No, not the one here with me leaning against a tree with a throbbing head wound. I thought about the bigger situation: life. Being a Texas Ranger had wrought changes in me. A life of riding the range, hunting, fishing, and raising a family was wonderful, but so different from where I was now. I had grown more watchful and suspicious of people.

I had enemies whom I didn't know and likely didn't know me, though they were obviously prepared to stop at nothing to kill me. I had friends like Buffalo Watts who came and went serendipitously, but not any close, true friends that I'd hunt and fish with. Of course, there were Cassie and the children and my mom and dad, but that was different. My dad thrived on hunting down lawbreakers on his own, though he had his Comanche friend One Eagle backing him up. The elderly Watts was no One Eagle. So, do I tell Captain Hughes that I've gotten as far as I could or pursue the case to its end? However, that letter that was worth killing for had me leaning toward finishing this case.

I fell asleep. When I awakened, it was to a starlit night. Tornado was close by. My stiff and aching body didn't want to move, but I was determined to stand. I was hungry, and there remained only two pieces of jerky in my saddlebag. New Braunfels wasn't far away, and I needed to resupply with guns and ammunition. There'd surely be someplace I could grab some grub.

Tornado eased on over to me and nuzzled my shoulder. I grabbed the saddle horn, planning to swing myself up into the saddle as I always did. It wasn't happening. I sighed. "Tornado, lie down." The big stallion lowered himself to the ground, where I could ease into the saddle. "Tornado, up." We were ready to ride.

The sleep had helped me to pretty much get my head together. I rode around the scene of the ambush. Other than tracks of two horses besides than Irma's and mine and a couple of shell casings, there was little evidence to go on. There were also boot prints around where I'd been lying. Other than worn heels, they revealed little. I sure wasn't going to pursue the bushwhackers until I was re-armed. "Let's get to New Braunfels, big fella." I headed us north.

THIRTEEN
PREY VS. PREY

NEW BRAUNFELS WAS A LOVELY TOWN. The town had become a manufacturing center for wagons, fine leather goods, farming implements, and more. As with many growing towns in Texas, the railroads helped fuel their growth.

After the better part of the night and early day in the saddle, I was headed up the main street when I came upon a white clapboard house with a doctor's shingle out front. I was hungry and tired, but knew that I needed my head wound examined. I nearly fell from the saddle, but was able to hitch Tornado and find my way up the walk to the front door. I rapped hard enough that I experienced just a touch of dizziness.

The door swung open, and a little bald-headed man looked up at me with caring eyes. "You look like you could use some help, young man," he said.

I sensed we'd get along just fine. "I'm Texas Ranger Lucas Dunn, and I've been bushwhacked."

"Well, come on in and let's have a look," he invited.

I stumbled a bit, but the doc caught me.

The doc guided me to a table and had me lie on my back. Soon, he was going to work removing my bandage. "You did a right fine job of treating yourself, son."

I sort of appreciated his compliment. "Guess I was lucky," I said.

"Oh, you were lucky all right. Another inch and you'd be gracing an undertaker's table."

"I much prefer living above the snakes," I responded.

The doc laughed. "Guess the bullet didn't hurt your sense of humor."

"I'm headed to Austin."

"You based out of there?" asked the doc, as he finished cleaning and began to rebandage my head.

"I'm with Captain John Hughes' Frontier Battalion," I replied. The doc was friendly, but a little too nosey.

"I guess the Texas Rangers will reimburse me," said the doc with a chuckle.

"You've done this sort of thing before?" I asked.

"More times than I dare keep count. It's still a tough land, Ranger Dunn." He paused in his bandaging. "Are you by chance related to..."

I laughed. "His son. They call me Junior."

"You tell your Texas Ranger friends that they still owe me for treating your dad."

With the bandaging complete, I swung my legs over the edge of the table and sat up. Naturally, my head spun, but I pulled myself together.

"You need to take it easy for a couple of days. Have you eaten anything?"

"I am hungry," I replied.

"Nice little place up the way that serves a great breakfast." The doc gave me an appraising look. "You might stay overnight. Come on back tomorrow and let me have another look at that wound before you head to Austin. Can't let you get infected."

I bade the doc farewell and took his advice as to breakfast. I was famished.

I took the doc's advice and caught a couple of days of much-needed rest in New Braunfels. I thought about contacting the county sheriff, but decided there'd be no benefit. Little did he know he'd missed the chance to house Irma in his jail for a couple of nights.

The local general store was well-stocked, appropriate to being part of a town that resupplied adventurous folks heading west. I used the good faith and credit of the Texas Rangers to purchase a new .32 caliber Smith & Wesson with plenty of ammunition and a Winchester carbine just like the one taken from me. I also bought ammunition. I bought some venison jerky while I was there. If business in Austin went as planned, I'd be headed back through here in a couple of days.

Once replenished, I saddled up and began the journey to the state capital at Austin. Now, I had time to think about my attackers. Not knowing who they were or who had hired them gnawed at me. Just as I was pursuing someone, I was also being pursued. It was a case of prey versus prey. It harkened back to my days hunting with my dad and Buffalo Watts. As a hunter, you were careful to not become the hunted.

I recalled the two key elements of the letter that had been stolen from me. The Railroad Commission of Texas stationery was one. Importantly, I recalled who had signed it: Leland P. Weatherby. What was his role in this? Would he live to tell? This railroad business was destined for hell. In fact, it seemed like a railroad to perdition.

My hat mostly hid the bandages wrapped around my head. My head no longer swam with each jostle of my trusty steed. About every hour, I walked Tornado for a while. It relieved my posterior and gave him a break from carrying my frame. Even pushing hard, Austin was a two-day ride.

We stopped to cold-camp for the night at what I gathered was the Blanco River. If the two who'd dry-gulched me had any idea that I was still alive, they very well could be on my trail. I was ever on guard. The venison wasn't half bad, and cold coffee was better than none at all. I decided that I'd do a bit of back trailing in the morning just to be sure I wasn't being shadowed.

A distant train whistle awakened me. It had rained a little during the night, but I'd sensed the weather change and had the foresight to cover myself with my rainslicker. I was mostly dry and yearned for some hot coffee and a hearty breakfast like I'd had back in New Braunfels. The distant train served to remind me of my mission. Dare I risk a fire? Hot coffee sure would be right fine. I filled my canteen, gathered my bedroll, and was soon doing that back trailing I'd promised myself.

There was a rise off to my west, a gentle reminder that I was headed to the edges of the hill country. I didn't ride to the very top, as I didn't want to serve as a silhouetted target if someone was on my trail. It did give me a vantage point.

I saw nothing and was about to turn north to resume my travels, when my eyes caught two riders. From the way they occasionally paused to study the trail, it appeared that they were tracking something. Then, I realized that they were on my trail. They must have heard about me in New Braunfels. If they looked at the letter and could read, they knew I'd be headed to Austin. They were nothing if not resourceful killers. As with many lawbreakers, they were smart but not smart enough. They didn't count on me being experienced enough to back trail. Now, roles had been reversed. It was prey versus prey, except I had now become the hunter. They outnumbered me, but I reckoned I could even those odds right quickly.

I eased Tornado down the rise and picked up their trail. Soon enough, they would come upon my campsite. It would be what I jokingly referred to as an *uh-oh moment*. They would realize that they'd become the hunted, the prey.

They dismounted at the spot where I'd camped and began nosing around, looking for my trail. About the time they caught Tornado's hoofprints back trailing, it was too late. They heard me chamber a round in the Winchester, as I sat my saddle a mere thirty feet away. "You boys looking for something?" I asked matter-of-factly.

Their mouths gaped. The bigger of the two reached for the Colt Peacemaker on his hip. It was a bad move. He hadn't cleared his holster when my bullet ripped through his chest. His companion froze.

"You want to try?" I hated having to kill the one and wanted this one alive. I needed some answers.

"N-n-no," he pleaded, as I saw the crotch of his pants become wet. He'd peed himself.

What a pathetic excuse for a hired gun. "Who are you?"

"Butler," he replied, looking nervously at his deceased companion. "George Butler."

"Who's paying you, Mr. Butler?"

"H-h-he knew," he replied with a head motion toward the dead man.

"Do you have the letter?"

"In his pocket. It's in his pocket."

"Fetch it, but be careful. Bullets are getting expensive these days." I urged him to get the letter.

He threw up as he reached into the dead man's pocket and drew out the letter.

What a sorry excuse for a human being, I reckoned. "Give it here, but real slow-like. My finger has a terrible itch. It can't stand human vermin."

The man sort of waddled toward me like most would with soaking wet pants. He was about to hand the letter to me when I caught sight of his free hand going for his gun. I should have disarmed him. Dang, but I was getting ever more careless. The muzzle of my rifle exploded in his face before he could clear leather.

I dismounted and grabbed the letter. I stuffed it in my pocket. I looked at the two dead bushwhackers. They did possess rifles of a caliber that matched the shell casings I'd found back where they'd dry-gulched Irma and me. However, once again, my sources had met death before I could learn who was paying them. It was frustrating, but it made me more determined than ever. I aimed to arrive in Austin by late afternoon. I looked at the two men. Their bodies lay askew in the rain-dampened grass. I thought back to how they'd left Irma and me for the buzzards. I turned Tornado northward and gave him a serious set of heels to his flanks. I wasn't wasting the time of day burying these lowlife thugs.

FOURTEEN
FRUSTRATION ABOUNDS

AUSTIN LOOMED in my sights just as the sun was beginning its final descent behind the hills of the western horizon. I was nearly salivating with anticipation of meeting Mr. Leland P. Weatherby. Then, I realized I was hungry. I didn't feature a first meeting with this Weatherby character on an empty stomach.

The sun cast an orange glow on the dome of the State Capitol. It was right pretty; majestic even. I decided that since the Texas Rangers were footing the bill, I'd earned a night at the Driskill Hotel. I rode up to the front door. Grabbing my saddlebags and Winchester, I turned Tornado over to an official-looking stable boy.

The Driskill was a drop-dead beautiful hotel. Anyone who was anyone lodged at the place at one time or another. The dark wood paneled walls and collector-quality art alone stood as testaments to the fine taste of the owners.

With two days of trail dust to my credit and a bandaged head, I strode up to the registration desk. "I'm Texas Ranger Lucas Dunn, and I need a room for tonight," I announced to the clerk.

The clerk gave me an appraising once-over. "Hope you won't be needing that, sir," he said with a judgmental look at my carbine.

"Don't figure to," I assured him. "I've got business here in Austin. I'll thank you for that room."

"We don't accept Texas Ranger promissories," he advised.

I let that sweep over me. "You ever meet Archer Parr?" I name-dropped.

"Mr. Archer Parr?"

I nodded.

"I'll ring him, sir."

Now, there was some luck. Archie Parr was coincidentally visiting here in Austin.

The clerk returned with an official-looking smile spread across his face that oozed sycophant. "He's expecting you, sir. Room 308." He smiled again. "Any bags, sir?" The little horny toad knew better.

I took the elevator to the third floor and soon found myself face-to-face with Archer Parr. "Why Junior Dunn! What brings you to Austin?" Despite past suspicions, I always judged Parr to be a good man. However, I sensed that politics was increasingly leading him down the path of corruption. He gave me a once over, wincing as he saw my bandaged head.

"Been on that railroad case I mentioned a ways back, Archie. I need to meet with someone here in Austin tomorrow and reckoned to spend a Texas Ranger dime at the Driskill."

"Guess they dissuaded you of that," he responded with a laugh. "Come on in and set. You're welcome to spend the night here. You can sleep on the sofa." He motioned to a coffee setting on a side table. "Help yourself." He sauntered over and sat in an easy chair near the sofa.

The room was amazing. Decked out in Victorian style, I almost hesitated to touch anything for fear of breaking it. My big frame didn't lend itself to this sort of fancy décor. I set down my saddlebags and rifle, poured myself a cup of coffee, and sat on the sofa across from Parr.

Parr slowly sipped his own coffee. "Mind sharing who you're meeting with?"

I shrugged. What had I to lose? "Leland Weatherby," I offered flatly.

I was nearly hit with coffee spray. "Weatherby!" exclaimed Parr. "Good Lord, how did you learn about that sonofabitch?"

This wasn't exactly the reaction I'd anticipated, if any. "Found it on a letter written on Railroad Commission of Texas stationery."

"A letter? You still have it?" he inquired.

"Yes. And somebody wants it badly enough to kill for it. Bland Olson stored it in a secret vault."

"Olson?"

"He's dead," I said. Digging in my shirt pocket, I produced the letter. At this point, I reckoned it couldn't hurt. I handed it to Parr.

He read it and read it again. "Whew! This goes so low, they have to look up to see hell."

"Pretty much what I figured, Archie," I said sort of resignedly. "By my count, this has already cost nearly a dozen lives. And every time I discover the next link up the chain, the fool gets himself killed. King Callahan, Bland Olson, hired guns, even Irma Callahan. Damn, but they bushwhacked me and left me for dead." I sipped some coffee. "I'm thinking of this as the railroad to perdition," I added with a chuckle, though there was nothing humorous in the situation.

"You now understand why I've stayed clear of the railroad business, Junior," he noted.

"Technically, I've solved the case in terms of who did the shooting. I've shot and killed three hired guns. Unfortunately, I wasn't able to find out who paid them, though I had my suspicions."

"Somebody wants to bring the Southern Pacific to heel," observed Parr.

"Seems that way," I said with conviction. "I visited with Uriah Lott, but this isn't his style. He's more a promoter. I don't think there's a sinister bone in his body."

Parr rubbed his chin thoughtfully. "Be interesting to see what Weatherby has to say." He paused. "If you get to him before someone kills him, too," he added ruefully. He stood and strode over to the bar. "I need something more than coffee," he said, as he poured himself a shot of whiskey. "Care for some?"

"I'll pass, thanks."

"I'm ordering dinner to be sent up. You hungry?" he asked.

"Twist my arm," I replied.

"A steak will cure you of any ills, Junior," he said with a laugh that belied his concern.

With the sunrise, I took time to enjoy breakfast with Parr. He called Weatherby's office and told them to expect me. We chatted briefly about ranching around Nueces and Duval Counties. I bid him goodbye, thanking him profusely for his hospitality and wishing him the best on his next political adventure. I reckoned to see Weatherby and head back toward home. I did take advantage of the telephone in Parr's room to call Cassie and tell her that I was all right and would be home soon. I even talked with Sean. He was thrilled just to hear my voice. After I hung up, I couldn't help but think about how he came within an inch of not having a father to talk with.

I found my way to Leland Weatherby's office. The building was an impressive sandstone edifice reflecting the power of the commission that seemed ever more inclined toward dabbling in oil than railroads.

I soon found myself walking toward the rich-looking mahogany door to Weatherby's office. A tall man wearing a gun and a cowboy hat stood at the door. As I approached, I saw his Texas Ranger badge. Mine was in full view, so I expected no trouble, though I was curious as to why he was guarding the door. "Howdy, I'm Lucas Dunn of Captain John Hughes' Frontier Battalion. I have an appointment with Mr. Weatherby."

"You're expected," he said, then paused with a doleful expression. "But you're late."

I gave him a curious look.

He elucidated. "Rangers are searching for evidence in Weatherby's office. He was shot and killed about an hour ago."

I was incredulous to say the least.

"I'm Phil Johnson. We understand that you're on this railroad case, Ranger Dunn." He wagged his head dismayingly. "You've sure found yourself a nest of rattlers from what we've heard."

"Heard?" I asked.

The guard laughed. "Get yourself an Austin newspaper," Johnson chided. "The press is having a field day with the story."

"Am I named?"

Johnson mulled that over for a moment. "Not that I know of. They just report that the Texas Rangers are on the case."

This news was a relief in a perverse sort of manner. Frustration seemed to build upon frustration, as the chain of command disappeared before me. I figured it was time for me to contact Captain Hughes as to what to do next. I wasn't going to catch him by telephone, so I aimed to send a telegram to Brownsville.

As to the present, there seemed to be no point in hanging around Austin any further. My detective work had reached a dead end—for now.

FIFTEEN
HOMEWARD BOUND

ARCHER PARR WAS generous enough to loan me a few dollars for supplies, so I bought food, bandages, and ammunition. It seemed no surprise that I heard nothing back from Captain Hughes. He was likely patrolling the Rio Grande with no access to modern communications. Eventually, my telegram would reach him, but it could take days or weeks.

Other than getting home safely to my beautiful, loving wife and children, I had no incentive to hurry. Of critical importance was arriving at Heaven's Gate safely. I could do it in about eight days, if I pushed. One upside of taking a little longer was that it gave my head wound more time to heal. I didn't feature showing up at the big house and having Cassie open the door to a man with a big bandage wrapped around his head. Perish the thought.

Heading southward, I figured to be passing through sheep country around Kyle and San Marcos and on to New Braunfels. The rolling hills in later summer were picturesque, though pretty much the same mile after mile. Tornado was a patient companion. I camped one night along the Blanco River and got an early start. My sleep had been interrupted twice by baaing sheep and barking dogs, so I figured the coyotes and wolves must have been active. I was a lot more comfortable when I reached cattle ranch territory. The lowing of cattle was a lot more preferable to my ears. I suppose it's about what we grow up with.

In a way, I missed being on guard for Garth Jones. Playing hunter and hunted with a hired gun had a level of excitement and challenge not offered by the likes of bears, mountain lions, bobcats, wolves, and the like. Jones was a thinking man's predator. The image of the naked gunfighter as my bullet plowed through him was one I'd not soon lose. It got me thinking as to what might be next. What enemies did I have lurking out there? At what bend in the trail was the Grim Reaper going to be reaching for my reins? Intuition told me that I wouldn't have all that long to wait. I was probably considered a loose end so far as these railroad men were concerned.

It was my fourth night on the trail home, and I'd skirted wide to the east around San Antonio. I camped alongside Cibolo Creek.

It occurred to me that Buffalo Watts hadn't crossed my path in a while, though that should neither have surprised nor concerned me. He was very much his own man, enjoying the freedom of a range that was ever less free.

Dad and Watts always said to pay attention to your senses. If you sensed something wasn't right, well...pay attention. I built a small cooking fire and enjoyed jerky and hot coffee along with a four-day-old biscuit. It was nothing fancy for sure, and Cassie's home cooking was ever closer. I let the fire die out, all the while feeling as though I was being watched.

Darkness took over. Clouds obscured what little light the moon and stars could shed. The craftiness in me, along with that all-important intuition, caused me to fluff up my bedroll and find a reasonably comfortable spot just inside the edge of a stand of live oak. Once my eyes adjusted to the darkness, I could see my campsite fairly well. After about an hour, a coyote stopped by and sniffed about. Something startled him, and he trotted away. I heard a thud as a rock was thrown and landed near my bedroll. I heard footsteps running away and then a horse trotting off into the distance. I stayed where I was, though I was dying to know what the rock was about.

The morning brought a light drizzle that I didn't much appreciate. Tornado still stood where I'd tethered him. He sent a nicker and a snort or two my way. I arose and stretched out my muscles, discomforted by the danged rocks I slept upon. I recalled the rock tossed into my campsite and ambled over to my bedroll. It had a note wrapped around and tied with a black ribbon. For a second, I thought it was a revisitation of Garth Jones and his taunting notes. I untied the ribbon and read the note.

"I aim to kill you, not your bedroll." Whoever he was, the fellow had a sense of humor. I looked around but saw nothing suspicious. Was this man going to tease me like Garth Jones had or simply ambush me? This was getting tiresome. Who was behind this?

I gnawed on some jerky. I dearly craved hot coffee, but my head wasn't into building a fire. I satisfied myself with water from Cibolo Creek. I took a tour of the area around my campsite. There were fresh boot prints, and a spot fifty or so feet away where a horse had been tethered. There was nothing notable about any of the prints. My foe would have been an easy target had he gotten closer to my bedroll. Seemed he had some smarts. I reckoned I'd find out whether he was up to his chosen profession.

Saddling Tornado, I mounted up and was soon on my way. Most any cluster of cactus or clump of grass could be hiding this new enemy. I was getting into country that I knew quite well from my hunting days with my dad and Buffalo Watts. Rather than take a straight-on southerly route, I headed eastward toward Stockdale. From there, I'd head toward Floresville. Hopefully, I'd fool my pursuer. My most critical challenge was that, as yet, I had no idea what my foe looked like. I had to find a way to get him to expose himself.

If he was smart, he'd realize that I'd eluded him. He'd go back to Cibolo Creek and try to pick up my trail.

Just west of Stockdale, I found a stand of live oak high enough on a hill to offer a great vantage point for surveilling the trail. Patience seemed to me to be the toughest virtue, but I was going to have to endure it. I tethered Tornado and decided to do a bit of taunting myself. I took a rock and wrapped my foe's note around it. I laid it in plain sight in the middle of the trail where I'd ridden. With a devious smile, I climbed the hill and took a reasonably comfortable seat under one of the larger live oaks. A couple of hours passed, and sunset wasn't far off. I wasn't to be disappointed.

A lone rider dressed in black was slowly following Tornado's hoofprints. He wore black pants, shirt, boots, and vest topped off with a black derby featuring an eagle feather. He would ride along with his eyes to the ground and occasionally scan his surroundings. He was tracking something. Me.

He saw the rock. I was close enough to read his face. He recognized the rock and had no need to read the note.

"Looking for something?" I challenged. I'm sure he heard the lever action on my Winchester.

The man froze.

He looked like a child caught with his hand in the cookie jar. He'd underestimated me, I dared not sell him short. "You might want to lose those guns, my friend."

He dug his spurs hard into his horse's flanks and was off like a shot from a cannon.

I swung the Winchester around and got off a shot that went way wide. Best I could say for the encounter was that now I knew what he looked like. Traveling would necessarily slow down, however, as I'd have to take the time to watch my back trail.

I made my way to a spot I knew of, just west of Floresville, on the banks of the San Antonio River, and set up camp. If my pursuer was on my trail, I had another great vantage point to keep an eye on my surroundings. I built a fire about fifty yards downstream, using damp logs to encourage plenty of smoke. Then I hid behind a big hillock of prairie grass a few feet back from the river.

Now, plain old dumb luck came into play. My foe dismounted and began creeping with his rifle at the ready along the riverbank toward the smoking fire. I reckon he figured he had me. Well, he walked past me so close I nearly could have reached out and touched him. "Drop the rifle. I'm Texas Ranger Junior Dunn, and you're under arrest."

The rifle dropped with a thud.

"Raise your hands and turn slow like," I ordered.

His arms had just started to go up when he spun around while simultaneously going for a gun at his waist. He reached it, but not quickly enough. He'd pulled it about halfway out when my bullet plowed through his upper arm. It's force thrust him back and caused him to lose his gun. Reaching for it with his good arm, he tripped over a root and fell hard on the wounded arm. After a scream of pain, he sat staring up at me with a totally evil look in his eyes.

Seeing him up close, I recognized him. "Johnny Jenks. Well, I'll be!" Jenks had built a reputation for robbing banks and trains. The train folks must have caught up with him.

"I ain't goin' in alive, Dunn," he snarled.

"I thought you were in New Mexico. Someone must be paying well. Who might that be?"

"Damn it, Dunn. I'm bleedin' to death here." His busted upper arm hung loosely at his side; his shirt sleeve already soaked with his blood.

"Tell me who paid you, and I'll give you something for the arm, Jenks."

"Don't know. Got cash and a note."

"Do you expect me to believe that? You've stepped up a notch from robbery to attempted murder. Who paid you?" I could see Jenks' face becoming ever paler from loss of blood.

"I only know it were train people," replied Jenks.

I sighed resignedly. If he bled out, I'd never get my questions answered. "I'll get a bandage. Don't you move a muscle." I backed away toward Tornado while keeping Jenks in my sights. I looked at my saddlebag for but a second, and a bullet whizzed past my ear. Jenks still had a pocket pistol. Thankfully, I was beyond its effective range.

Jenks tried to get off a second shot while trying to stand. It missed.

I did some quick mental calculations. I decided that he'd been telling the truth that he had no idea who paid him. I levered a round into the Winchester's chamber, aimed, and put a hole dead center in Jenks' chest. He fell in a heap.

I began rifling through Jenks' pockets and saddlebags. I finally found an envelope full of cash. I counted nearly a thousand dollars. I was about to toss the envelope, when I saw *Railroad Commission of Texas* printed on it. Someone was careless or trying to cast blame. I corralled Jenks' horse, hoisted his body over the saddle, and tied him in place. It occurred to me that there might be rewards on him in New Mexico. I made a mental note to myself to check that out.

There was yet enough daylight to take the body to Floresville. I was about to do just that when it crossed my mind that turning him in might alert whoever had hired him to the fact that I was still alive. Having his poor horse spend the night with a dead body on his back seemed rather unkind, so I untied Jenks and hung his body over a live oak limb. Hopefully, the horses and I would be near enough to discourage scavengers. After several days of considerable concern, it was wonderful to get a decent night's sleep.

Waking up at dawn, I checked the body first thing. It didn't smell very pretty, but it had not been attacked by buzzards or coyotes. I wrapped Jenks in his bedroll blanket and once again tied him over the saddle. If he smelled so foul this morning, I reckoned he'd be quite putrified by the time I reached Kenedy later today. Nevertheless, that's where I was determined to deposit Jenks. I couldn't account for the man's soul, but the body was mine to dispose of.

It was great to be back on my journey home. I was beginning to salivate in anticipation of Cassie's home cooking. I'd been working this case for about four months and

simply couldn't feel satisfied with having found and eliminated the murderer of the railroad workers. Solving those
killings had been the case, as we'd understood it. It had
evolved into so much more. Would Captain Hughes want
me to keep at it, given how it had grown? Texas was now
littered with the bodies of folks connected with the case. I
had almost become one of those bodies.

I looked forward to depositing Jenks' body with Sheriff
Brack in Kenedy. He undoubtedly had a collection of
wanted posters I could peruse to see whether there was a
price on Jenks' head. A few extra dollars would be nice to
spend on gifts for Cassie and our children. I wondered how
Sean was making out with the puppies. Puppies? What was
I saying? Brody and Tess would be darn near full-grown by
now. I wondered whether they'd remember me? No worry,
dogs don't forget.

Sheriff Brack wasn't overly pleased with the condition
of the body I turned over to him. He did permit me to look
over his file of posters. He was an organized man and had
them sorted by state. That made it a might easier for me. As
luck would have it, there was a modest thousand-dollar
reward for Johnny Jenks. I had Brack draft a receipt and
copy for Jenks' corpse and sent the copy off to Santa Fe.
Hopefully, some money would show up for us in a few
weeks at the Alice National Bank.

SIXTEEN
PERDITION

WITH HEAVEN'S Gate close but a week's ride ahead, I reflected on the mysteries surrounding this case that Captain Hughes had plunked me in the middle of. Hell seemed to have broken loose. The railroads created huge opportunities, and that drew big money and powerful people. It was like a bunch of giant moths being drawn to a raging flame. In this case, it seemed to be the flames of hell itself. I mustered a grim smile and muttered in Tornado's ear, "It's a railroad to perdition, big fella." Yes, that's what it was, a railroad to perdition.

I decided to board a train there in Kenedy. I was plumb tired of riding and reckoned that the train might give me some wild and crazy ideas toward solving the mystery behind all this murderous chaos. Of course, the train was nothing new to me as I'd ridden one a few months back up to Fort Smith to consult with Bass Reeves. A different purpose now lay before me.

The train that steamed into the Kenedy Station looked to be brand spanking new. Fresh black paint glistened in the midday sun as the iron horse belched steam across the platform. It stood there huffing and puffing. Passengers disembarked while others boarded. I saw to settling Tornado in a freight car provided for that purpose.

As I left the livestock car and prepared to board a passenger car, what I saw as I glanced off to my left caused me to pause in mid-stride. It was some sort of executive coach, and it oozed money. The words Southern Pacific were emblazoned on its side. Between the car I'd be occupying and the coach was a flatbed car that enabled a clear line of sight. I couldn't help but wonder who was occupying that palace of the rails? Was there a connection with the railroads? I looked again. A heavily armed guard stood vigilantly on the forward observation deck. I presumed another stood at the rear. Something or someone of value required a guard.

Well, there's nothing like something unexpected to further roil a mind already stirred up over a bunch of murders. I took a seat, being careful to lean my Winchester toward the window. The seat opposite was unoccupied, so I seized the opportunity to prop my feet on the cushion. I was right comfy. My cogitations on railroads and murders and executive coaches soon lulled me to sleep.

"Ticket please!" said the ticket agent, interrupting my nap.

I allowed one eye to peek from beneath my hat and reached into my pocket.

The man in his neat railroad-issue uniform punched my ticket, thanked me perfunctorily, and moved on.

I was wide awake. Stretching, I scanned the car to see whether I might be traveling with anyone of note. Two women were seated near the front. Men occupied the remaining seats, with four unoccupied. I couldn't miss the fact that four of the men were impressively armed, not unlike the guards on the executive coach. I reckoned they likely served as relief for the two men on duty. All of this was a bit of a distraction from my original purpose for boarding the train.

One of the men shot me a threatening look, then backed off when he spotted my Texas Ranger badge. I laid a couple of fingers beside my hat brim to acknowledge and adjusted my position to better see out the window. The passing scenery was nothing special, as most of the countryside was rolling hills populated by tall grasses. Now and then, I spotted cattle, sheep, and horses. Fields of cotton also spread across parts of the landscape.

The train would be taking on water just outside of Beeville. I sat as unobtrusively as I could, observing the changing of the guard. I looked over my shoulder and was able to see the coach through the windowed doors at the rear of the car I was riding in. For the briefest of moments, I saw a well-dressed man talk with a guard. A woman stood behind him but quickly disappeared into the coach. Now, this was getting truly intriguing. Was there any chance that whoever was on board that executive coach might know of the goings on with the Railroad Commission of Texas and the clash between the Southern Pacific and SA&AP Railroad?

I could hear the boilers gathering pressure and the train readying to pull out, so my chance to investigate the coach might be Skidmore. Tornado and I would be leaving the train at Sinton, so I would only get one chance.

My thoughts churned the elements of my railroad to perdition case over and over. There had to be a mastermind behind the entire chaotic mess. It wasn't long before the train had Skidmore in its sights. I could feel the brakes as the engineer slowed the locomotive for its approach into the station. I reckoned that I wouldn't have tons of time to engage the coach occupants. Moreover, there would be the guards to deal with.

As the train came to a halt at the Skidmore station platform, I grabbed my Winchester and was striding quickly ahead of the shifting guards. In fact, I was a good half a train car length to the coach before the first guard stepped onto the platform and headed my way.

"Hey, you!" called the guard behind me. "Where you think yer goin'?"

I made it to the coach before he could catch up to me. The guard on the front observation deck had just stepped down, and we came face-to-face. By this time, the guard behind me had caught up.

"Thet badge don't git yuh nothin' special, Ranger." Said the guard in front of me.

"I'm Texas Ranger Lucas Dunn of the Frontier Battalion, and I'd like to meet your employer." I used as professional a tone as I could muster.

"Don't care who yuh are," replied the guard. He turned to what were now two guards behind me. "Sam an' me, we be escortin' this man back tuh the train," he stated.

The guard from the rear observation deck now appeared, so I was dealing with four hired guns. I gave my best aw-shucks look. "Now, gents, I'd just like to meet your employer. I'm working a case, and he might be able to help." Up the tracks, the train gave its first warning whistle. It'd be pulling out in a couple of minutes. The guards looked to be immovable objects, although they seemed reluctant to lay hands on me. I wasn't about to get physical either. This was a standoff. Just as I'd decided to back off, I saw a woman's face appear in the executive coach's side window.

But a moment passed, and the well-dressed man I'd seen earlier appeared on the forward observation deck. "What's the matter, men?"

The man referred to as Sam looked up. "This here Texas Ranger was lookin' tuh board yer coach, Mr. Giles."

I noticed that the train had apparently been ordered to stop.

Giles looked down at me. "You are?" he asked.

"I'm Texas Ranger Lucas Dunn of the Frontier Battalion, sir. I'm on a case involving the railroad and wondered whether we could chat."

The guards looked up expectantly at Giles.

"Ranger Dunn, I have my daughter with me and am busy with papers. Perhaps another time would work." Giles passed me a card. "Make an appointment, and I'll be pleased to meet with you."

I was simultaneously encouraged and disappointed.

Giles smiled and disappeared inside the coach, while the guards motioned me back to the passenger car. Two of the guards and I barely made it back to our seats before steam belched, a whistle blew, and the train lurched from the station. The guards and I exchanged smiles. I suppose it qualified as semi-professional courtesy.

I turned Giles' card over in my hand. I'd make an appointment. I hoped he'd still be alive. Here was a man who'd had the sense to hire guards, so he must have been leery of all the mayhem that was going on around him.

Now, I found myself in a fine how-do-you-do. I desperately yearned to spend time at home with Cassie and my children. On the other hand, my duty as a lawman pursuing a case was to fulfill my commitment. Another concern was whether Landry Giles would still be alive when I eventually landed an audience with him. Time and duty had a boot on my neck and were pressing hard. This case had already taken far too long, so far as I was concerned.

I eased myself down onto the station platform in Sinton and took a final look back at that fancy executive coach. The woman identified as Giles' daughter had stepped onto the forward observation deck and was looking at me. She smiled. I smiled back at her, turned, and headed toward the car in which Tornado had been riding.

It took a while to settle Tornado after his ride on the train, but I was soon saddled up and we headed south toward Nuecestown and then on to Heaven's Gate. With any luck, a telegram from Captain Hughes would be awaiting me.

While I remained cautious, I was of a mind that whatever price had been placed on my head was not getting a return on the investment in hired guns. They might back off...then again, perhaps not. It was like a dark cloud hanging over my head. As I thought on Giles and his guards, it did occur to me that, if he were involved in anything sinister, he could have set his guards on me. Of course, that might have been a tad too obvious in broad daylight. I did keep a wary eye on my back trail.

The ride from Sinton took about a day. I encountered only a couple of innocent-looking enough travelers as I wended my way home.

My ride through Nuecestown caused me to think back on stories my dad told of violent encounters around the little town's environs. Today, it didn't appear that Nuecestown was thriving. It seemed to be hanging on to economic success by a mere thread. It had been the scene of the notorious Good Friday Raid back in 1875, when Mexican bandits ostensibly from Juan Cortina swept the landscape with killings, lootings, and burnings. The bandits kidnapped a bunch of locals, including some of my Dunn cousins.

A posse of ten men was led by my cousin Pat Whelan and including Texas Ranger John *Red John* Dunn and his brother Matt Dunn. The posse drove off the bandits and rescued the hostages unharmed. One posse member, George Swanks, was killed. I was fascinated by the story my dad told of the theft of Noakes saddles and how for years afterward any Mexican subsequently caught with one of the prized saddles was summarily dispatched.

Today was a long time since the raid, but the town had changed very little. A few more folks had undoubtedly been added to the cemetery, and a new schoolhouse had been added. The old general store, jail, boarding house, stagecoach inn, smithy shop, and doctor's house had gotten ever-older with time. The place desperately needed a railroad stop if it was to survive. It would be ideal if Uriah Lott ever built his St. Louis, Brownsville, and Mexico Railroad.

I was soon sitting atop Tornado's back, looking up at the archway to Heaven's Gate. Dame Fortune had shown upon me, and I'd arrived safely. Tornado needed no urging. I reckoned there was a mare or two that was on his mind.

We eased on up the lane toward the big house. I reined in about fifty feet from the front of the house. Cassie was sweeping the gallery while Sean played in the dust with the puppies Brody and Tess. Baby Bode sat in a chair made special for him, so he would stay occupied while Momma did chores. I took in the sweet aroma of life. Suddenly, Sean looked up. I'd been discovered.

"Daddy!" yelled Sean.

Cassie dropped the broom and snatched Bode from his chair.

I'd barely slipped from my saddle when Sean and the dogs were latching onto my legs. A moment later, Cassie was hugging me with Bode crushed between us. This could only be called a joyous homecoming.

Cassie stepped back and took a long, hard look at the scar alongside my head. I'd only ditched the bandage a couple of days before, and there was no way of hiding the wound. She stared at it for the longest time, then smiled. She leaned in and kissed me.

I ruffled Sean's hair and took Bode from Cassie as we climbed the stairs to our home. As I stepped through the threshold, I felt Tornado's eyes following me. "Come on, we've got to go to the barn," I announced. I'd been shamed into a most necessary chore.

We walked Tornado to the barn. His ears were pricked up as he snorted and whinnied all the way. I gave him an extra special currying. I even held Sean while he got in some strokes with the brush. A few loving strokes of his forehead and a bucket of feed completed the care of my awesomely loyal steed. Cassie watched all of this with a bemused smile, as though fully appreciating her family.

"You hungry?" asked Cassie on the way back to the house.

I wrapped an arm around her slender waist. "For you," I teased.

Cassie went about whipping up some dinner while I played with Sean and the puppies. Brody and Tess seemed to have enough energy for everyone. Bode cooed happily on a blanket nearby.

We finally sat down to dinner, and I must say it was one of Cassie's best ever. Yes, I'm prejudiced, but her cooking would stack up well against the very best.

"Captain Hughes stopped by two days ago. He asked that you visit him in Corpus," said Cassie with a certain reserved tone. She had gotten a tad tired of this case, especially so now that I'd been shot. Being a lawman's widow wasn't in her life plan.

SEVENTEEN
VISIT WITH THE BOSS

I FIGURED that there was no point in delaying the inevitable. With a promise to Cassie that I'd take a few days off after meeting with Captain Hughes, I saddled Tornado and headed for Corpus Christi. My beloved Appaloosa stallion wasn't all that excited either, as he longingly looked at the mares prancing about in the pasture.

The road to Corpus was now quite well-trodden. It carried a rich history, which my family had been an integral part of. Pondering that history segued into the case at hand. What would my lawman ancestors have done? I knew that my retired Texas Ranger cousin Red John Dunn lived near Corpus, so I resolved to stop by for a visit. From what I knew, he was a tough hombre who seemed inclined to deliver justice more with from-the-hip action than careful planning. Nevertheless, he might have a helpful idea.

I was roughly halfway to Corpus when I saw a rider approaching. He looked vaguely familiar.

"Junior!" the rider called out as we drew closer.

Well, turned out it was my old friend Kyle McClintock. I

hadn't seen him in about eight years. "McClintock, you rascal. What brings you this way?"

"Could ask the same," he replied. "Haven't seen you in a coon's age, Junior. Hear you joined up with Hughes' Frontier Battalion."

"I'm headed to the city to meet with him." We sat there silently, facing each other. McClintock had visited Heaven's Gate a time or two when we were teens and helped punch cattle. We'd become friends. He fancied himself a suitor for Cassie, and I'd never been quite sure whether he ever got over my winning her heart. "What are you up to?"

"I've got a horse deal in Alice," he answered. "Sure wish they'd get these railroads figured out. They make travel so much faster."

"Amen to that, Kyle. I've been riding the rails a bit lately." He had no idea how ironic my statement was.

"How has it been following in your dad's footsteps?"

I laughed. "Folks get over it."

"Cassie doing well?"

"We have two young-uns now, plus a pair of dogs. Heaven's Gate is thriving."

"I finally got hitched," added McClintock. "You remember Mary Anne Dougherty?"

"Lovely lady. Sure do," I was pleased that he'd married. You never really get over hanging with someone who fancied himself a rival for your woman's attentions. "You get finished up in Alice, do stop by the ranch." We laughed a bit, shook hands, and rode on.

It had been good to meet McClintock, and I resolved to renew our friendship.

★★

Upon arriving in Corpus Christi, I hitched Tornado in front of the hotel and headed inside. I checked at the front desk for Hughes' room number. I was about to head upstairs when the clerk stopped me.

"Pardon, Ranger Dunn, but he's dining over yonder in the restaurant."

I looked out across the street. I wasn't able to make out the patrons, but I reckoned I'd head on over. I was unsure as to what to expect, as I unhitched Tornado and walked him across the street. I tied Tornado's reins to the rail, hitched up my big boy pants, and strode on in. I let my eyes adjust to the dim light and soon focused in on Captain Hughes. Surprise of surprises, he was seated with none other than Landry Giles. What was this about?

Hughes spotted me and pulled a third chair to the table as he motioned me over.

Giles gave a smile of recognition and walked over.

"Glad you're here, Ranger Dunn," said Hughes as I grabbed a seat. "I understand you and Mr. Giles have met."

I smiled and nodded toward Giles. "The circumstances were a tad unusual," I noted.

"I wasn't taking any chances about arriving here in one piece," he stated. "I knew that you were investigating the railroad matter, but couldn't let on to that little assembly of guards."

"Well, Mr. Giles, I expect you saved me a trip to Austin," I said.

Hughes scanned the room. There were two elderly couples seated a few tables away. "Mr. Giles has a thought or two about this case, Ranger Dunn," he said in a near whisper.

The young lady serving tables came by with fresh coffee. She refilled Hughes' and Giles' cups and added one for me. "You having lunch, cowboy?" she asked.

"Not just yet, thanks kindly," I said by way of sending her away. I turned back to the matter at hand. "My guess is that you're figuring to keep me on this case, Captain," I commented to Hughes.

He nodded. "No point in repeating the facts of this case thus far," Hughes noted and turned to Giles. "Please repeat for Ranger Dunn's benefit what you shared with me," he enjoined.

"I've spent the past few years as a financial executive at the Southern Pacific's San Francisco headquarters. Some ledgers were brought to my attention by one of my staffers. I reviewed them and came upon what appeared to be a bit of skullduggery in Texas concerning the San Antonio & Aransas Pass Railroad that we'd acquired from receivership. That brought me to Austin and thence to San Antonio, where I ran headlong into the murderous goings on that Ranger Dunn here has been investigating."

This seemed straightforward enough to me. However, the lingering question was who was engineering the scheme and why violence was resorted to? I looked at the captain.

"Go ahead, Ranger Dunn. Speak freely but not loudly," Hughes counseled.

"Do you have any suspicions, Mr. Giles?" I queried.

"Roger Mills took John Reagan's US Senate seat so Reagan could head the Railroad Commission of Texas. I suspect that Mills and Reagan have something cooking," postulated Giles.

I took a long sip of coffee. Some pieces of the puzzle were being brought together. "It invariably boils down to someone seeking to be in control. But to the person in control, it tends to be a hollow victory, absent of friendship and love with loyalty bought with gold."

Hughes looked at me as though seeing me for the first time. "Dang, Junior, you nailed that."

Giles smiled. "I appreciate your wisdom, Ranger Dunn. However, making a case against these railroad titans is a tall order. You need help at a high level, and it dare not be me."

I wondered why not Landry Giles, but who was I to question? "What's your thinking, Captain?"

"I've been so tied up with disruptions on the Rio Grande that it was all I could do to break away at Governor Culberson's direction. Mexicans and Apache have been raising holy hell. There's been talk of assigning Rangers to go undercover, but talk is all there's been." Hughes looked at my expectant expression. "It wouldn't work for you in any case, Junior. You've become too well known."

The good news and bad news was that I had gained some notoriety. "Undercover likely isn't the answer, Captain, though I've been trying to think, as some say, outside the box. The information about Miller and Reagan that Mr. Giles has provided gives credence to some thoughts I'd been having about this case. It became ever clearer that someone at the top was working the strings of the marionettes. I had my nose so tight to the trail, it was hard to see where it was headed."

"I doubt you'd ever get to see Reagan at his office, Ranger Dunn. However, I'd be up to luring him out into a social setting where you might just happen to meet him. That's about as far as I dare go. I suspect that my life is already at some risk, and my daughter doesn't appreciate that."

I nodded. Folks tended to be upset at risks to the lives of their loved ones. Cassie sure appreciated that sentiment. "Do you have something specific in mind?"

While Giles mulled over possibilities, I hailed the server

and pointed to the lunch special on the chalkboard beside her. She nodded and scurried to the kitchen.

"I could throw a party at the Menger in San Antonio under the auspices of the Southern Pacific. My daughter and I could host."

"When?" I pressed.

"I'll have to work that out. Sometime in September, I would think," postulated Giles.

"You might have to dress up a tad, Junior," teased Hughes. "It might do to bring your wife."

Giles smiled. "I could have a special train arranged for you."

I began to envision Cassie and me all dressed up in our Sunday-go-to-meeting clothes and attending a social gathering in the big city. I had seen a dress in Corpus Christi that would suit Cassie spectacularly. She'd be the belle of the ball in purple satin that would set off her long reddish-blond locks. Of course, I'd have to invest in some new clothes for myself.

"What do you think, Junior?" asked Hughes, interrupting my musings.

I smiled. "I think it just might work. We'll have to come up with a leading question or two for when I meet Mr. Reagan. They must touch on the case without being overly intrusive. It wouldn't do to offend the man in public."

Giles nodded. "Then we're set."

The server placed a platter of steak and potatoes in front of me. The steak was obviously cooked to perfection; rare just short of mooing.

Giles and Hughes looked at my plate and motioned the young lady to whip up the same fare for them.

"Sorry. I thought y'all had eaten," I said bashfully.

"Just coffee and some bear sign," noted Hughes. "It was

seeing that delicious-looking steak that made us realize that we were hungry."

All was forgiven as to food.

"You've been doing a great job, Ranger Dunn. I know it's been a lonely and dangerous assignment." Hughes was making certain that Giles heard his plaudits about my performance. "I understand that you even took a bullet."

We made light conversation through lunch. As the meal was ending, Hughes made a motion to me that it was okay to leave.

I cleared my throat and took a final sip of coffee. "Gentlemen, if y'all will excuse me, I promised my wife that I'd be home by this evening. It seems we have a plan. I'll look forward to hearing from you, Mr. Giles."

I shook hands with Giles and Hughes, nodded friendly-like to the server, and headed out. I reckoned the meal was compliments of the Texas Rangers.

As I went to mount up, I saw a familiar cayuse. It looked an awful lot like the one I saw Kyle McClintock riding earlier in the day. What was he doing back here so soon? I thought about seeking him out, but felt compelled to stand by my promise to Cassie.

I headed for Heaven's Gate and my beloved Cassie. I reckoned to spend at least a week and maybe a bit more at home. My dad wasn't feeling great. His old bruises and wounds had gradually been catching up with him. I thought of him like my rancher cousin Nick Dunn, who was sixty-two and going strong. Dad was roughly the same age, but his legendary career as a lawman had taken its toll. My mom was toughing it out, but recognized that the end might be in sight.

EIGHTEEN
THE PARTY

I RODE STRAIGHT on into the barn. The dim light of dusk had settled over the landscape, and a lantern had been hung on the door to help guide me in. I was brimming with news to share with Cassie, including a shopping spree in Corpus Christi.

With meeting Landry Giles and receiving assurances from Captain Hughes, I'd rejuvenated my pursuit of this case. The railroad to perdition case would be resolved soon. I was sure of it.

I settled Tornado, grabbed the lantern, and headed for the big house. The sun had sunk below the western horizon, and it turned out that I was especially glad to have that lantern. I'd taken but a few steps toward the house when the buzz of a rattler caught my hearing. The snake was not more than six feet in front of me and was a big one. My Smith & Wesson made short work of the fanged reptile, though it took two shots to finish him off.

The gunfire brought our ranch hands from the bunkhouse and Cassie to the gallery railing. I waved off the ranch hands, then picked up the rattlesnake and headed for

Cassie's welcoming arms. This wasn't a very romantic picture, which I was quick to realize. I dropped the snake and swept Cassie into my embrace.

She nestled her face into my chest, as the puppies pranced at our feet. "Welcome home, Ranger," she murmured into the folds of my shirt. "I've been saving a spot for you upstairs," she cooed.

Over the next few days, we rustled the bedsheets a few times. Cassie fed me far too well. My diet during the weeks chasing the railroad case had left a lot to be desired. Cassie was appreciative of my leaner, well-muscled frame. However, I wasn't enthused about chasing lawbreakers and getting shot at to maintain it.

Our mailbox was graced with a gold-engraved invitation to a party hosted by the Southern Pacific Railroad. Hosted by Landry Giles and his daughter Carolina at the posh Menger Hotel, the railroad executive had been good to his word.

"The weather should be lovely on October 7, Lucas," said Cassie as she sat beside me and read the invitation. "I'm sure your mom or mine will be overjoyed to watch Sean and Bode."

"They might have to take turns," I said with a laugh. "Even taking the train from Corpus, we'll be away a couple of days."

Cassie batted her eyes playfully. "What shall I wear?" she said with a Texas twang.

"I expect we need to get ourselves to Corpus and find you a dress, sweetheart," I invited. "I saw a purple silk dress in one of the store windows. It sure would set off your beauty."

Cassie smiled. She was hearing the words she loved to hear.

To look at her, you'd never know that she'd birthed our two boys. Her slimness with curves in the right places sure kept me interested. "Let's head to the city tomorrow," I suggested.

I hitched up the carriage, and we all headed to Corpus Christi. I did tether Tornado to the back of the rig just in case. I was still concerned about bushwhackers. I reckoned my being with my family wouldn't matter a hoot to many of them.

Sean sat between Cassie and me, while the pups took in the fresh air from the back seat of the rig. I'm sure we made for quite a sight.

Blessedly, the journey was mostly uneventful. I say mostly, because I did see my old friend Kyle McClintock resting his horse along the Nueces River. We exchanged waves. I wondered why he kept showing up after so many years of not seeing each other. I wanted to believe it was plain old-fashioned coincidence. Why was it beginning to concern me?

We arrived midday in Corpus, and I headed our rig directly to the Cacti & Boots, the store where I'd seen that purple dress. The place was owned by Scarlet and Walker, old friends of my mom and dad. As I pulled up, I stared at the window. Oh no! The dress was gone! I said nothing to Cassie but helped her and the kids down from the carriage and led them into the store.

"Where's that dress you mentioned, sweetheart?" she asked.

I shuffled my feet a bit. "It's not in the window any longer. We'll have to see what they have."

Cassie nodded. "You need a new suit, too."

I appreciated that she was thinking of me. After all, we needed to be presentable as a couple. I hailed the store clerk. It turned out to be our old family friend Walker Carson. "Pardon, but do you still have that purple dress that was in your window a week back?"

Cassie and I both looked at him with hopeful anticipation.

Walker smiled. "Great to see y'all. Your father was in here the other day. He looked to be ailing a bit, but his mind sure was sharp. He bought some goods for the ranch and some niceties for Elisa." He paused. "Scarlet decided to swap out that purple dress. She's got it in the back." His eyes scanned Cassie. "It just might fit you with no adjustments," he added, raising his eyebrows with a sense of assurance. "Go ahead and try it on. Scarlet is back there."

"What about you, Lucas?" he asked.

"I expect you'll have to do your level best to turn me into a fitting partner for my beautiful wife," I said with a laugh. "I'll need something with enough hip room for my Smith & Wesson."

"I've got the perfect coat, Junior. It's got a special interior compartment that ought to be a fit for that Smith & Wesson."

Carson had just begun to show me the way to the men's suits when Cassie appeared wearing the purple dress. My mouth dropped. "Wow!" I exclaimed. She looked amazingly beautiful. The dress reached the floor and featured puffs of cloth at the shoulders and a couple of black ermine highlights along with sequins. She literally lit up the Cacti & Boots haberdashery. "What's that?" I added with a sideways glance at something she was holding.

"It's called a parasol, sweetheart. It goes with the gown." She paused with a demure smile. "Or, do you prefer the fan?" She opened a fan and fluttered it under her chin.

Little Sean was toddling through the store, as each aisle became an adventure for his senses. Brody and Tess sniffed about like puppies do and did their best to stay out of trouble. I must say that we'd brought the store to life.

"We'll take them all," I announced. "Oh, how about shoes?"

Cassie stuck a toe out from under the gown. "Like these?" The shoes Scarlet had selected wrapped her feet in sparkles and helped set off the gown.

"Come on, Lucas," called Carson. "Let's get you outfitted." He paused. "You're a big man, but I may have a suit that fits. The coat has that compartment I mentioned."

Soon enough, we were outfitted and began to bid our goodbyes. There was a candy jar near the register. I looked down at Sean and recalled my folks buying me treats, when I was a little shaver. Cassie gave me a slight shake of her head, as if to say Sean was too young. That didn't stop me, as I added some treats to our purchases.

We rode over to the train station. I reckoned to purchase our tickets in advance. As I hopped from the carriage and stepped up to the stationmaster's window, I caught sight of McClintock's horse hitched near the smithy shop. Much as I had good memories of him from my teen years, these coincidences were beginning to bother me. I hoped I wasn't dealing with another Garth Jones situation.

I went to pay for the tickets, but the stationmaster had recognized me. "A Mr. Giles said you'd be along, Junior. The tickets are on him." He handed an envelope to me.

"Thanks kindly, Bill." I accepted the tickets and opened the envelope on the way to the carriage. There was a note inside. Senator Miller would also be at the party. This was looking to be a great opportunity to break the case. I hoped that my railroad wasn't actually headed to perdition.

It was near dark when we turned up the trail into Heaven's Gate. If McClintock was following me, I never saw him.

The party in San Antonio was set for Saturday, so we planned to leave the day after tomorrow. We'd take the carriage and carefully pack our dress-up duds. This time, the boys, puppies, and Tornado would be left behind in the care of their grandmothers. They were overjoyed at the opportunity.

I did strap on my Smith & Wesson and hauled the Winchester along. With all that had happened with this railroad case, I wasn't up to taking chances. It didn't seem to bother Cassie any, as she was growing increasingly excited about hobnobbing with the elites of San Antonio.

We were roughly three-fourths of the way to Corpus Christi, when I spotted a familiar face coming our way.

"Wahg! How you folks doin' this here fine day?" called Buffalo Watts.

I pulled the carriage up beside him. "Where you headed, Buffalo?"

Watts laid a concerned expression on me. He looked apologetically at Cassie. "Kin I bend yer ear a minute?"

I caught Cassie's eyes. They said okay, so I stepped down and walked a few yards away with Watts. "What's the bother?" I asked.

"There be a fella followin' yuh."

"Kyle McClintock?" I responded.

"Thet be him. We had a bit of a talk," said Watts.

"You didn't hurt him, did you?" I said with concern.

"Not yet. He's up to no good, Junior. Some fool's payin' his sorry ass. I think I persuaded him to stay clear."

I didn't want to believe what Watts was telling me, but put together with so many McClintock sightings, it made some sense. "He admit anything?"

"It was in his eyes, Junior. The tell always be in the eyes." Watts smiled. "Watch yer back," he advised.

"Thanks, Buffalo."

"You two enjoy yer trip," he said, waved to Cassie, and headed up the road.

I climbed back into the carriage and took the reins. I was silent.

"What did he have to say, Lucas?" Cassie asked.

I wanted to not mention Watts' warning, but that wasn't our way. We were always honest with each other. "He said someone was paying Kyle McClintock to follow me," I stated flatly. "He said to be on guard."

"Kyle was always the friendly sort, Lucas," Cassie replied. Her eyebrows were knitted a tad with concern.

"Money can change folks, sweetheart."

"You think he'd shoot you?" She said flat-out what was on her mind.

"He never was much of a marksman," I said, trying to laugh it off.

Cassie forced a smile as she tried to absorb my assurance. "The party will be exciting, Lucas." She deftly changed the subject.

Kyle McClintock was nowhere to be seen. My suspicion was that Watts had thrown the fear of the wrath of God into the erstwhile spy. It was most likely at the point of a knife.

★★

Cassie thoroughly enjoyed the train. From the power of the locomotive to the clickety-clack of the cars on the steel rails, the experience played with her senses.

We were surprised in the dining car, when we were served champagne compliments of Landry Giles. The man was laying out the red carpet for us.

The ballroom of the Menger was all aglitter. Cassie and I stood for a moment surveying the scene before us. I felt my Smith & Wesson revolver nestled in a reinforced pocket within my coat lining. I'd likely not need it, but it did afford a sense of security. A band was playing dance music at the far wall, and folks in server uniforms ran about with food and drink. I had a fleeting memory of my previous visit to the hotel with Irma Callahan. What a contrast! I looked down at Cassie. She was radiant in that purple dress, and she had a fluid manner with the fan. There was a certain allure to her motions. I suspected that Scarlet had taught her.

Cassie and I glided in arm-in-arm. I spotted Landry Giles with his daughter Carolina, sipping champagne and talking with a gentleman who looked important.

Cassie looked up at me, having caught my look of recognition. "That must be your Mr. Giles."

"Might as well get on with this," I said aloud and led Cassie over toward Giles.

"Why, Mr. and Mrs. Dunn," exclaimed Giles, friendly-like. "Welcome to our celebration. We've saved a couple of seats for you at our table over there."

"Good to see you, Mr. Giles," I said in my best solid Texas Ranger voice.

Giles turned to the gentleman beside him. "Lucas, it's my

pleasure to introduce you to John Reagan, head of the Railroad Commission of Texas." He turned back to Cassie and me. "John, these fine folks are Luke and Cassie Dunn. They own a big spread down near Corpus Christi. I think they're trying to outdo that Kleberg fellow down in Kingsville."

Reagan extended his hand, and we shook. "A pleasure to meet y'all." He paused. "Your name sounds familiar," said Reagan.

"You may have heard of my father," I responded.

"No," he said flatly. "I've heard your name a couple of times. Are you connected with the railroad?" Reagan didn't waste time with conversational niceties, though I suspected he was trying to simply make a connection.

"Luke here is also a Texas Ranger, John. He serves under Captain Hughes." Giles figured there was no point in my ties to law enforcement being revealed later and Reagan feeling deceived.

Reagan nodded. He was about to say something, when a bell sounded announcing dinner.

"I expect we should mosey to our seats, ladies and gentlemen," urged Giles.

As we approached our table, I caught a glimpse of Archer Parr in my peripheral vision at another table. He sure did get around political animal that he'd become.

The band began to play dinner music, as servers scurried about delivering the first course. Champagne flutes were being filled around the room. Giles had seated me beside Reagan, while Cassie sat next to Carolina. I noticed that there was an empty seat.

"Senator Miller will be joining us," said Giles upon seeing me notice the empty place.

"Have you heard anything about these terrible goings on along the old San Antonio and Aransas Pass line?"

asked Reagan. The man apparently did not mince words when he had something gnawing at his mind.

I nodded. "Yes, sir. I'm aware of it."

"Nasty business," he said with an apologetic glance at the ladies.

We engaged in some friendlier conversation about ranching and the growing oil business. To his credit, Reagan engaged Cassie and asked about our boys.

We were just a minute into the main course, when Senator Miller arrived. He apologized for being late, and Giles made the necessary introductions. Miller and Reagan greeted each other like long-lost family.

Giles gave me a look that told me that he'd dealt the hand, and it was up to me to play the game.

I smiled and nodded.

As the meal drew to a close and coffee was served, I turned to Cassie. "I'm going to have a chat with Mr. Reagan, sweetheart," I whispered.

"I believe I'm going to head to the veranda and enjoy fresh Texas air and a smoke," said Reagan with a nod to Miller.

I chuckled inside at the contradiction of fresh air and smoking. "Mind if I join you, gentlemen?" I stood. Admittedly, my six-foot-four-inch frame rather dominated the space.

Reagan nodded. "Sure. Come along."

Giles waved us off. "I'm keeping these beautiful ladies company."

"How many head on your spread, Luke?" asked Reagan. He offered me a cigar, which I politely turned down. Miller accepted the offer, and smoke soon invaded our little bit of airspace.

"Just a couple of thousand beeves," I responded. "My father's ranch adjoins ours, so we mix herds a bit. Figuring to be raising quarter horses next year."

Reagan looked off at the starry night. "How much do you know about the murders, son?" Again, the man didn't hold back.

"I eliminated the shooter," I said matter-of-factly. I looked from Reagan to Miller and back. They appeared nonplussed. "It remains to figure out who paid him."

Reagan and Miller exchanged knowing looks. Reagan sighed. "The Southern Pacific is a haphazard mess, Ranger Dunn. It's built and bought its way to dominance of the southwestern routes. Hard to believe that the product of four Sacramento merchants has achieved so much. Leland Stanford, Mark Hopkins, Collis Huntington, and Charles Crocker pulled the Central Pacific together based on a transcontinental model conjured up by a fellow named Theodore Judah. They initially purchased what was then the Southern Pacific from a fellow named Phelps. It ran down the coast from Sacramento to San Diego. The four partners set their sights eastward. As you've already experienced, the process has been fraught with all manner of skullduggery."

"But who?" I interrupted.

"Hang on, son. Let John finish," interjected Miller.

"There was and still is big money involved. Your friend Landry Giles has uncovered a lot of unsavory financial deals. He rightly fears for his life." Reagan took a long pull on his cigar. "I suspect you've been targeted, too."

I nodded.

Reagan and Miller exchanged knowing looks. "There's

eastern money at play, Ranger Dunn," said Reagan. "Texas, too," he added.

"I'm looking to cut the head off the snake, Mr. Reagan," I said. "But it sounds like that mythological Hydra with many heads."

Miller smiled at my reference. "More like Medusa. Folks who figure it out get turned to stone."

"Gordon Murphy is the man you want to talk with," revealed Reagan.

"Who is he?"

"The commission is keeping an eye on him because of his interest in oil, but he's a financier who moved from New York City to Dallas about five years ago. He represents millions of dollars. He's been making essential connections in Texas." Reagan took another long pull on the cigar. "He's intent on controlling the railroads as part of creating a huge power base in Texas."

"Why are you telling me this?"

Reagan and Miller glanced at each other. Miller took a long pull on his cigar, while Reagan put on an uncharacteristically furtive smile. "Leland Weatherby was a good friend of ours," lamented Miller.

"And?" I pressed.

"I've folded my hand in this game, Ranger Dunn," said Reagan. "I've got to maintain a clean image with the Railroad Commission of Texas or it loses any remaining credibility."

Miller shrugged. "Bottom line is, we don't want to end up like Weatherby. He was getting close to going to the press about Murphy."

"Aren't you at considerable risk standing here talking to me?" I asked.

"The streets are crawling with hired security, Ranger

Dunn. I doubt anyone can see us, much less get close enough to shoot," said Miller with confidence.

"I saw my dad shoot a coon at eight hundred yards. One shot; dead coon."

The two men's confidence seemed to waver slightly.

On a blind hunch, I asked, "Either of y'all acquainted with Irma Callahan?"

Senator Miller blinked. "Callahan? That tramp was bought and paid for by Gordon Murphy out of a Dallas bawdy house. None of us know her real name. She was a gift to King Callahan to ultimately grab his land for the railroad. Murphy aimed to start a new town with a rail line running right through it. King Callahan got in the way." Miller looked at me. "Do you know what happened to her?"

I nodded. "She took a bullet from me as she defended Garth Jones. I intended to protect her, but she was bushwhacked along the way to New Braunfels. Wounded me, too."

"A bit ironic," mused Reagan. "Murphy must be none too happy."

"There's a hired gun on my trail now," I added.

"Do you know who it is?"

I nodded.

"How's that?" asked Miller.

I smiled. "I have folks watching my backside, Senator."

"The band's playing some dancing music, gentlemen," enjoined Landry Giles as he strolled onto the veranda. "You best not disappoint the ladies." There was a certain charm about Giles. Perhaps, it was a San Francisco thing.

"Gentlemen, thank you. I'll take your advice."

Reagan whispered in my ear. "You never spoke with us, Ranger Dunn."

I watched Miller and Reagan reenter the ballroom. Giles

and I exchanged knowing looks. "This is going to get interesting, Mr. Giles," I understated.

"Go dance with your wife, Ranger. The men in there are slobbering over her."

I didn't need to be asked twice. Cassie and I were soon swirling around the dance floor to the envy of the men and even of the women. I was surely dancing with the Queen of the Ball.

After more dances than I could remember doing short of our wedding day, we returned to our table. Giles and his daughter were cooling off from dancing. She had suffered through the toil of dancing with several partners; most of them awkward stumblebums. Miller and Reagan were nowhere to be seen. For that matter, I recalled having seen Archer Parr earlier in the evening, but we never connected. He seemed to have slipped out as well.

Cassie and I sipped the last of the champagne and it was late. "Mr. Giles, thank you for your hospitality. You've been a wonderful host." I helped Cassie from her seat and made a small bow to Carolina. We reckon to head to our suite."

"We'll be headed back to San Francisco tomorrow, Junior. I hope this has been a profitable evening for you." He stood to shake my hand and secretively passed a folded piece of paper to me.

"I'll be sure to let you know, sir," I responded. I didn't look at the note but stuffed it in my pocket.

Cassie and I headed for the exit. We looked forward to relaxing in our suite. Giles had gone all out for us, and I found myself pleased with the result.

With Cassie on my arm, we approached our suite on the third floor. As I went to insert the key, a sixth sense caused me to pause. Any residual effect of champagne disappeared. "Stand back," I whispered to Cassie.

She gave me a fearfully curious look and stepped aside behind me.

I drew the Smith & Wesson from my jacket compartment and stood aside as I inserted the key in the keyhole. I made it scrape the keyhole a couple of times to make some noise.

The air instantly exploded as three shots blasted in rapid succession through the door. There was a thudding of feet inside the suite, the sound of a window opening, and then silence.

I put my hand up to warn Cassie to stay where she was. "Don't move," I whispered with enough authority that she'd dare not move. I unlocked the door and pushed it open. I could see curtains blowing in the breeze. It appeared that someone had escaped out the window. I cautiously walked over and waved my hat outside before sticking my head out. We were three stories up. There was no ledge. Where had the shooter gone? I heard the scrape of a boot on the floor behind me. I turned, aimed, and fired in a mere heartbeat. The expression on the shooter's face was one of utter surprise as he fell forward, landing face down in front of me. "Stay out there, Cassie," I called.

I examined the dead man. It was no one that I recognized. I patted him down. There was no identification. I picked up the room phone.

The desk clerk answered. "Yes, may I help you?"

"This is Mr. Dunn in room three oh eight. Please send someone up here. We need some trash cleaned up."

"Trash, sir?"

"Yes. You'd better bring a laundry cart," I insisted. With the danger passed, I had found a bit of levity in this situation, but there was a job to be done. Keeping a sense of humor in this lawman business was often an essential part of preserving our sanity.

"Right away, sir," responded the clerk.

I hung up. "Come on in, sweetheart."

Cassie eased tentatively into the room and immediately saw the corpse lying in the middle of the room. "Oh my, Lucas!" she exclaimed.

"Room service is on its way. I need you to go into the sitting room while I handle things here."

At the knock on the door, Cassie dashed into the sitting room.

I strolled casually over to the door. Two Mexican women stood at the door with a laundry cart. I didn't want to alarm them. I gave a relaxed smile and brandished six gold pieces. "*Esta basura nunca debe ser descubierta.*" I said distinctly and firmly while patting the Smith & Wesson they could see inside my coat. I told them that this trash must never be discovered.

"*Si, señor,*" they assured me.

We dumped the body into the laundry cart and covered it with some dirty towels. By morning, someone would be going nuts trying to figure out what happened. Where was the dead body of Texas Ranger Dunn?

With the women gone and the door shut and locked, I coaxed Cassie from the sitting room. "Do you want me to request another suite?" I asked tenderly.

Cassie gave me a look I'd never seen before. She glanced at the bloody residue where a carpet had been. "Cover that." She pointed at the floor, then gave me the most wanton look I'd ever seen. "I want you right this minute." She let down her hair and began to slip out of her beautiful purple gown.

I barely got the blood stain covered and my coat and pants off before Cassie was ravaging me. Her hands and lips explored my body. Her mouth took me in, and then she mounted me and brought herself to the heights of orgasmic climax. Just when I thought she was fulfilled, she began again. We couldn't keep our hands off each other. Our lips melted, tongues explored, passions knew no bounds.

We awakened wrapped in each other's arms. Dazed and with a weird sense of humor, I wondered how many hired guns I'd have to kill to have a repeat performance of last night. Of course, I didn't dare say that to Cassie.

She opened her eyes and batted them at me. "You were wonderful last night," she cooed.

"You weren't half bad yourself," I teased and rolled on top of her. Our passions were quickly renewed.

We regretted having to leave the hospitality of the Menger Hotel behind, but we did need to get back to the ranch. We missed the children and pups. The short ride to the train station was uneventful, and we were soon speeding on the rails toward Corpus Christi.

Despite Cassie's cuddling beside me, my mind drifted to just how I might go about setting a meeting with Gordon Murphy without getting myself killed. Meanwhile, had Buffalo Watts truly dissuaded Kyle McClintock, or was the man lurking out there to ambush me?

"Look, Mr. Texas Ranger." Cassie opened her blouse just enough to give me and only me a peek at her bounty. "Can't wait to get home, Lucas," she said with a soft sexiness.

I stopped thinking about Murphy and McClintock.

NINETEEN
THE PARR FACTOR

THE TRAIN RIDE to Corpus Christi was a swift one, and we were soon in the carriage heading to Heaven's Gate. The leads and cautions, combined with the secretive nature of my liaisons in San Antonio, coupled with the attempt on my life, gave me plenty of cause for concern. I was running with the apex hunters, and that was an exhilarating game played for keeps.

Cassie clung to me like barbed wire to a man's pants. She wasn't about to let her man go. Can't say that I was unhappy about that so long as my Winchester and Smith & Wesson were within reach.

We were trotting along about two miles from the ranch when I heard a shot about the time a bullet whizzed over our heads. I pushed Cassie to the floor beneath the driver's seat and snatched the Winchester. Shooting at me was one thing, but anything close to Cassie was a death sentence for some fool. I scanned where I judged the shot to have come from. Nothing.

I looked down, and Cassie was gone, along with my Smith & Wesson. She had climbed over the seat and was waving my gun around from the rear of the carriage, looking for the attacker. I'd nearly forgotten just how tough a woman she was.

"Keep an eye out," I called. I wasn't about to hang around and give some bushwhacker a second chance. The daylight was failing anyway, so I didn't make for an easy target. I scrunched down and snapped the reins to propel the team into a full gallop. They didn't let us down. I gave them their head and managed to rein them in just as we reached the gateway arch to Heaven's Gate.

I was seething over the ambush attempt. With all that was going on, the shot had not been some hunter's errant bullet. As we pulled up to the house with Cassie still crouched low in the rear of the carriage, I was already planning to revisit the bushwhacking scene in the morning.

The grandfathers had come to our house to help with the kids and puppies. My dad was looking a tad rough around the edges, but in good spirits. Despite our hair-raising experience, we were glad to see everyone, especially our boys. Sean and Bode about flew into our arms, and the puppies couldn't hold back their enthusiasm.

Our parents stood on the gallery laughing at the sight.

I gave them a curious gaze, then realized how we must have appeared arriving in the carriage in such unusual positions. I gently fended off puppies and boys and headed up the steps. "Some fool took a shot at us a couple of miles out." I shared solemnly. They all got serious right quickly.

Cassie came up beside me and slid the Smith & Wesson back into my holster while sending an innocent smile to our parents.

My dad gazed at me. "You finding trouble again?" he mused.

"Shucks, Dad, I'm no ground-hitched cayuse," I responded with a wink. Once a horse's reins have been repeatedly tied to stakes in the ground, it soon no longer becomes necessary to tie them. They just assume they've been hitched and never wander off.

The grandmothers set to work whipping up some grub. It wasn't a meal, but right tasty fare for such short notice.

We made small talk about the great party at the Menger, though I left out the business of my meetings with Reagan and Miller. I let on as to what a gracious host Landry Giles was, and how I learned more about the railroad business, per the case I was working on. Of course, I shared how beautiful Cassie had been in the purple dress. Oh, and I left out the ambush in our suite at the Menger. It wasn't something to talk about over a meal. I could tell that my dad sensed there was plenty more to tell. It was lawman talk, and I'd share it with the two dads later.

"One interesting thing," I floated conversationally. "Archer Parr was at the party. I never got to chat with him, but he was rubbing elbows with the moneyed folks of San Antonio."

My dad nodded. "That man's got some serious political ambitions, Junior. There's an old saying about keeping your friends close and your enemies closer. I'm not suggesting that Archie Parr will ever be your enemy, but I'd stay close with the man."

"I wonder whether he's getting an interest in railroads," I postulated.

"Harrumph, more like oil," said Cassie's father. "Your dad's right. Keep him in your sights."

"When you heading out again, son?" interjected my mom.

I looked over at Cassie. "Reckon to be around a few days. Lots of family catching up to do." I winked at Cassie. I had the sense that she was anxious to send off our folks and get the boys bedded, so she could bed me. There's an old saying about absence making the heart grow fonder, but Cassie's mind was way beyond fondness. Truth be told, mine was too.

The sun was heading for its meeting with the horizon, when the folks said their goodbyes. They'd enjoyed the opportunity to watch the boys and keep the puppies fed.

Cassie and I exchanged *that look*. Soon enough, the boys were bedded, dogs let out, and the bedroom in our sights. This time, I didn't have to kill a hired gun.

I rolled out early to take a ride across our spread. Aside from reconnecting with Tornado, I had plenty of serious thinking to do that didn't lend itself to making love with Cassie all morning. Landry Giles had given me the private address of Gordon Murphy. I had to muster a plan for how to go about meeting the man. It would surely take some surveillance, as I imagined the man had plenty of guards. I also gave thought to whether it would be worthwhile to visit Archer Parr. Was he a factor in all of this or just greasing his political aims? I figured to let my Parr concern rest for now.

I reckoned that speed was of the essence. My Texas Ranger duties aside, I feared for the lives of Giles, Miller, and Reagan. Would these power-mongers be so bold as to kill a sitting senator? Giles and Reagan were no less key to stopping Murphy and his minions, so they were surely in danger. I wondered how far did Murphy's tentacles reach? Who was he in cahoots with? While railroads seemed to be a key link, I had begun to realize that oil was the driver behind the murder and mayhem being spread across Texas.

That thinking brought me back to Archer Parr. His holdings were situated in oil country. Shucks, all of Texas seemed to be oil country. The oil business was worth millions of dollars. Little wonder they called it black gold. "What do you think, Tornado? It's about oil, isn't it?" I got a loud whinny for my rhetorical questions.

I spent the next couple of hours roaming the ranch, even freeing a longhorn bull that had been tied up in a fence. I lamented that barbed wire now stretched for miles, partitioning properties, as it protected water sources and grazing lands. Finally, I headed Tornado for home.

In a perverse sort of way and despite the inherent dangers, I appreciated that Captain Hughes gave me these cases. It beat being away for weeks patrolling the Rio Grande with a bunch of lawmen of widely disparate moral character and fighting ability.

We had ridden a mile or so, when I caught the glint of metal far off to the north. It was the sort of flash typical of a gun barrel. I gave fleeting thought to checking it out. I was armed but not bulletproof. I reluctantly turned Tornado a bit to the south to stay out of range. If it was Kyle McClintock, I took comfort in knowing that he likely couldn't hit the broad side of a barn even at close range.

With Tornado curried, fed, and comfortable in his corral, I strode up to the house. I now had to muster the courage to tell Cassie that I'd have to return to my Texas Ranger duties. I decided not to tell her about the distant threat I'd seen. There was no point in unnecessarily upsetting her with me about to leave.

I reckoned to take the train to Dallas, as it was faster than horseback, and Tornado had earned a break from long trail rides. I'd also save the Texas Rangers a dollar or two and stay at the City Hotel with its Mechanics Hall Saloon. Dallas was quite a bustling city with a population of around forty thousand these days. Cattle was king, making the city an interesting choice for Murphy.

I poured myself some coffee and slipped up beside Cassie, as she was bathing Bode. "I'll be headed out day after tomorrow, sweetheart. I've got to bring this railroad case to a close."

"Who? Where?" she asked with genuine curiosity.

"I did chat with those men that Giles wanted me to meet at the party. The man that's apparently causing all the mayhem is named Gordon Murphy, and he's holed up in Dallas."

Cassie shook her head. "Dangerous isn't it?"

"I can't sugar-coat it. He's going to be a tough man to get to."

"What about that bushwhacker?" she pressed.

"I'm sure it's McClintock. Buffalo Watts thought he'd scared him off." I lovingly stroked Cassie's hair and gave her a reassuring kiss. "He won't bother you. It's me he wants."

She shook her head in dismay. "You're just going to go out and ride into an ambush?"

"I'll deal with McClintock," I assured her.

Cassie toweled off Bode and handed him to me. "Bode and his brother aim to grow up with a father, Lucas Dunn Jr." Her intent was clear. Don't take unnecessary risks.

I set Bode on the table and hugged Cassie. "I reckon it'll take about a week to have everything cleared up. I'll be sure to watch my back trail." I said this knowing full well that Murphy surely had plenty of hired protection, especially with the knowledge that I was pursuing the case. The fact that Jones failed and now McClintock couldn't rein me in must have been frustrating to the man. I was convinced by now that Murphy was chosen for his take-no-prisoners attitude as an advance man for the eastern money that would pour into Texas.

Cassie looked up at me, and her eyes softened. Since I was headed out soon, it wouldn't do to get caught up in worry. She would be sure to have her way with me with renewed intensity.

TWENTY

DALLAS ADVENTURE

ON THE WAY TO catch the train in Corpus Christi, I stopped at my cousin Red John Dunn's place. Red John had gained considerable notoriety as a Texas Ranger under less-than-savory circumstances, though his star had shone brightly during the famed Good Friday Raid back in 1875. He was with the posse that freed hostages held by a gang of Mexican bandits and helped drive the revolutionary hopefuls back to Mexico. He was now enjoying the good life as a rancher and had begun to collect militaria from around the world as a museum he'd decided to curate.

I rode up the lane to his house. I'd ridden a chestnut gelding that hadn't been ground hitched, so I dismounted and tied the reins to an iron hitching post.

Red John ambled out into the bright Texas sun. "What brings you by, cousin?"

"Just passing through. Reckoned to pick your brain quick like."

"Ranger business?" he inquired with a smile.

I nodded. "Got one bushwhacker tailing me and about to head into a nest of vipers up Dallas way."

Red John thoughtfully twisted his handlebar mustache with his fingers. "Not sure I can help you other than advising you to be aggressive as hell. You need to get the tail off your back. I recall you being right good at back trailing."

He was right, and I knew it. I suppose I needed to hear it from someone else. "What about Dallas?" I pressed.

"You've got to work at night. Get the lay of the land as best you can. Where's your prey from?"

I liked hearing Murphy referred to as prey. That was how I needed to think of the man. He was naught but a hired thug. "I understand he hails from New York City."

Red John laughed heartily. "Shucks, Junior, you just have to throw some old-fashioned frontier justice his way." He looked at my holster. "That Smith & Wesson is right nice, but I'd get yourself a second one before you head to Dallas. You may need the firepower."

I hadn't considered the need for a second revolver. I suppose I'd resisted the image of being some sort of gunslinger like in the dime novels. "I appreciate the advice, cousin. I'll be sure to stop by after this case is finished. I hear you're putting together a hell of a collection."

Red John smiled and leaned his wiry frame against the gallery post, thumbs wrapped around his suspenders. "Be sure to watch your back, Junior." He gave a wave as I mounted up and headed off.

I checked my back trail a couple of times, but there was no sign of anyone tracking me. I also left the main road to frustrate anyone figuring to ambush me. Upon riding into Corpus Christi, I headed for the first general store I happened upon. I wasted no time purchasing a new Smith

& Wesson to match the one I had, plus I bought a twin holster rig to accommodate the two. I didn't cotton to stuffing a gun in my waistband. It was an uncomfortable way to carry and didn't give me any sort of safe feeling. Guess I feared an accidental firing of the thing.

I put the gelding up at a nearby livery and walked toward the train station. I had time to kill before my train departed, so I headed to a nondescript-looking place called The Palace Saloon to wet my whistle. Moving from bright sunlight to the dim interior necessitated a considerable adjustment of my vision.

Looking about, the place was like most other saloons in the city that featured an over-abundance of them. Dark wood furnishings in a room about twenty feet wide and sixty or seventy feet deep, with a dozen or so tables and some sort of stage at the far end, and featuring a bar about twenty feet long. I placed my foot on the brass footrail. I wasn't able to make out anyone that I knew at first scan of the place.

I eased up to the bar and hailed the barkeep. "Got a cold one?" I asked for a beer.

He nodded, glanced at my Texas Ranger badge, and managed to quickly set a mug of the cold brew in front of me. I stuck my lips in the frothy head and took a long swallow. Feeling more at ease, I took another scan of the saloon and its clientele. Two customers were sitting with their backs to me but appeared harmless enough. As I took a second swig of beer, someone emerged from the rear of the saloon. Danged if it wasn't Kyle McClintock.

McClintock spied me at the bar and nervously averted his eyes. The man was every bit the cowardly bushwhacker.

I thought this might be the end of it. We could both just walk away from this.

McClintock seemed to suck up his courage enough to

walk over and set himself beside the bar roughly six feet from me. It was too close and a move that took *cajones* for sure. It became clear to me that he'd been at least partially paid to kill me, and he feared those who'd paid him more than he dreaded me. I might be a Texas Ranger today, but his scrawny mind recalled us as teens and on a more equal footing.

"How much they paying you, Kyle?" I turned to face him and give him a full view of my guns.

"Don't know what you're talking about," he mumbled. He'd found the courage to approach the bar, but I could sense his knees weakening. He lacked sand. Worse for him, he looked to have had one whiskey too many. It'd given him a little false bravado.

The barkeep began to pay attention to our exchange, and I saw him move to a place where a shotgun was likely hidden behind the bar.

"That's not what Buffalo Watts told me," I persisted.

"Old fool should mind his business," responded McClintock. He turned to face me, and his hand began to move to the gun at his hip. His fingers touched the butt.

I'm not a fast draw artist, but McClintock suddenly found himself looking down the barrel of one of my Smith & Wesson revolvers. His eyes widened and his jaw dropped as his hand moved away from the butt of his gun.

"You dumb fool. Stay away from me! I see you again, I'll kill you!" I stepped forward and wrapped him up the side of his head with my gun. He fell out cold like a bag of rocks.

The barkeep froze.

I finished my beer and laid money on the bar top. I smiled at the barkeep. "When this man wakes up, tell him to stay away from Texas Ranger Lucas Dunn."

He smiled back and nodded. "Yes, sir," he said.

I made it to the station and boarded the train with my mind considerably eased. Hopefully, I'd dissuaded McClintock once and for all. Question was whether he'd be a dead man by my hand or whoever had hired him?

A few folks gave me a once-over, as I walked up the aisle and took my seat. Some seemed impressed, others fearful, and still others offended. The days of lawmen carrying revolvers gunslinger-style were heading for the dustheap of a past era.

I nodded politely to each and every passenger whose eyes I caught. This was going to be a long journey, so I figured we'd better get comfortable with each other. In fact, the train would cover the four hundred miles in about two days with transfers and water stops, while it would have taken me two weeks on Tornado. So far as the passengers were concerned, none of them raised my hackles as threats. Maybe Murphy was off his game or thought McClintock got the job done. Then again, maybe he was falling into the carelessness that often comes with overconfidence. In my limited experience, once a lawbreaker makes a mistake, more usually follow.

I pulled into Union Depot aboard a Houston & Texas Central Railroad train. I must say that I caught up on my sleep time and appreciated the stops along the way for the opportunities to stretch my legs. It was about as exciting as the gentle rocking of a saddle, only I arrived at my destination far sooner.

I didn't figure to be able to create a plan to corral Murphy until I got a look at where he lived and what places he frequented. Some dollars spent with locals would likely help. Call them bribes, if you will. Upon hitting the station platform and grabbing my satchel, I headed for the City Hotel.

Dallas seemed to stretch out as far as the eye could see. I had the address Giles had passed on to me, but had no idea where the place was. Shucks, I didn't even know what Murphy looked like. The City Hotel had the advantage of an adjoining saloon, so that would be a great place to start.

I checked in, cleaned up a tad, and headed for the Mechanics Hall Saloon. The clerk had given me the name of the bartender. I pushed my way through a pair of batwing doors and headed to the bar.

Bellying up to the bar, I made certain my Texas Ranger badge was in view. "Say, Ricardo," I called. "Is the beer cold?"

Ricardo smiled. This was a good beginning. Ricardo poured me a cold one.

I tipped back my hat, hung a boot on the brass bar rail, and casually scanned the room. Far as I could count, there were eight patrons. One stood at the end of the bar opposite me, the others sat at round tables in clusters of three and four. The foursome looked to be playing poker. Not being a gambling sort, I reckoned to stay clear of them. Nothing unusual caught my attention. But for the decidedly tough-looking cowboy at the bar, the others dressed as city folk. That is, they wore citified duds comprised of suits with vests and set off with one of those derby-style hats. I guess me and the cowboy were pretty much odd men out fashion-wise.

Ricardo was busying himself cleaning and rearranging glasses as though anticipating some sort of late afternoon rush of patrons. With six empty tables, there'd be plenty of room.

"Ricardo," I called.

"*Si, señor*," he said as he strode over to me. "*Cerveza?*"

Barkeeps were the not-so-hidden secrets of every western town. They possessed insider information on all that was going on. There was little that they missed, and they were often a lot smarter than folks gave them credit for. Perhaps, that's why folks told them dark secrets. Barkeeps were good listeners. What had Ricardo heard lately?

"*Bonito día*," I said.

He looked at me as though he'd expected me to ask for information. He'd likely been asked before by lawmen pursuing outlaws.

I decided not to disappoint him and laid a couple of gold coins on the bar. "You hear of a fellow named Murphy?" It was a broad question.

Ricardo's eyebrows raised at my question, and he looked at the coins. They were more than a tip for good service. "*Hombre malo*," he intoned.

I was being blessed with incredible luck. Here I was but an hour in Dallas, and the first person I approached knew of my quarry. I wasn't about to let up with my questioning. "*Cuántas armas?*" I figured to be so bold as to ask how many hired guns Murphy had.

"*Mucho. Quizás, veinte o más*," He said in a low voice. He shook his head. "*Muchos hombres malos*." His eyes looked furtively toward the cowboy standing at the other end of the bar.

I took notice that the cowboy was packing a .45 caliber Colt Army single-action revolver. That was heavy hardware for little old peaceful Dallas. "*Viene* Murphy *aquí?*" I pushed for a bit more and dropped another gold coin. Honestly, I wouldn't expect Murphy to hang out with his hired guns but had to ask.

"*Él no muere venir aquí, señor,*" confided Ricardo.

I suppose the saloon would have been swarming with hired guns, if Murphy hung out here. However, I sensed that there must be someplace that the man escaped to. "*Dónde,*" I pressed for a tad more.

"*Una casa cerca,*" said Ricardo with a smile. I sensed that he was enjoying this.

So, my prey hung out at a house nearby. That meant there were plenty of guards around...or were there? I thanked Ricardo and headed back to the hotel. It would have been senseless to ask the barkeep not to tell anyone I was here. The cowboy at the bar had already glanced my way a couple of times and noted my twin Smith & Wesson revolvers. The word would get to Murphy right quickly that the Texas Ranger was in town, if it hadn't already.

I lay in bed trying to relax but failing at that. How was I going to get to Murphy? I heard rain falling. The drumming of raindrops did have a calming effect. A flash of lightning and rumble of distant thunder let me know that the streets of Dallas would soon be a muddy mess not fit for man or beast.

I almost didn't hear the soft knock at my door. I grabbed one of my guns and tiptoed to the door. "Who's there?" I whispered.

"Open up," came a youthful voice.

I took a deep breath and opened the door a crack, sticking the barrel of the Smith & Wesson ahead of me.

"I'm Joey. Ricardo sent me." A boy of no more than ten years stood behind the voice. He glanced nervously at my gun. The boy was soaking wet.

I motioned him inside and threw a towel over him. "Ricardo sent you?" I wanted to be sure I'd heard right.

"Ricardo say you look for this bad man named Murphy."

I nodded. "You know where he is?"

For the first time, it occurred to me that if something bad happened, I had no escape. I was vulnerable. Nevertheless, this was a great chance to sew up this case.

"I take you," said the boy, pretty much ignoring the towel.

I sighed. It looked as though I was going to get wet, as I hadn't brought a slicker. That was the least of my worries. Could I trust this youngster to get past Murphy's hired guns? Had I any choice? The bright flash from a bolt of lightning lit up the room, and thunder shook the window. It was a pretty good setting for some dangerous intrigue.

I buckled on my guns and followed the boy from the room and down the hall. Blessedly, we were on the first floor, so we availed ourselves of the rear door. Conveniently, someone had snuffed out the lantern beside the door, so we stepped out into darkness and driving rain.

We crossed three rain-slicked streets. I saw no one, no passersby, no street traffic, and no armed guards. My young guide eventually had us standing among soaking wet shrubbery beside a shuttered, nondescript clapboard house. I could see light inside through the shutter slats and heard the faint sound of voices muffled by rain and the house wall.

"I leave," said the boy.

I couldn't blame him. He couldn't afford discovery or to be around if shooting started. I pulled out a coin, but he shook his head and was gone before I could insist.

I scanned my surroundings, especially appreciating when lightning lit up the area. I saw no guards. There was no time like the present to make my move. I made my way to the back door. I didn't reckon to knock.

I timed my kick for a peal of thunder that rattled the shutters. The door burst inward, and I followed with both guns drawn. There I stood, dripping wet, staring at a naked man and a young woman on a kitchen table in the midst of full-fledged fornication. I slammed the door shut behind me. "Pleased to meet you, Mr. Murphy," I said drolly. I suppressed an urge to laugh.

Murphy separated himself from the woman and stood with his hands over his privates, while the girl grabbed a dish towel and did the best she could at modesty. He was a tall man, but not nearly so big as I. His hair was graying. A neatly cropped mustache decorated his upper lip. "Who the hell do you think you are?" he snarled.

"Why, Mr. Murphy, I'm Texas Ranger Lucas Dunn here to ask you a few questions. Would you be so kind as to put on your pants and keep your hands where I can see them?" I remained calm despite the bizarre situation.

"How did you find me?" The red in his face contrasted nicely with his gray hair.

The woman moved to the door.

"Don't you go anywhere, miss," I advised. I tossed her Murphy's shirt from a nearby chair. I turned back to the Easterner. He didn't look like a powerful bigwig New York City financier at the moment. "It's taken a lot of time and effort to catch up with you, Gordon Murphy." I stifled a triumphant smile.

"If my men don't hear from me in fifteen minutes, you're a dead man, Ranger Dunn," threatened Murphy.

"Well, we don't have much time then, do we? You and the lady sit over there." I motioned to the chairs beside the table. Its surface was wet with a mix of rainwater and passions. "A lot of men and at least one woman have met their Maker by your hand, Mr. Murphy. I'm here to put an end to it."

Murphy flashed an evil smile. "You have no idea what you've gotten yourself into." He'd recovered from my surprise entry. "You won't leave Dallas alive." He snickered. "Pity."

I holstered both of my guns and pulled out my Bowie knife. "I like the knife for this sort of work, Mr. Murphy. Now, what are you trying to do here in Texas?" It was sort of a rhetorical question.

Murphy stared quizzically at the knife. There was another flash of lightning and more thunder. Closer this time.

"Don't you have these in New York City?" I teased.

"What are you going to do?" For the first time, a hint of fear crossed his face.

"I'll begin with your lady friend here. Maybe take turns depending upon your answers."

"You're crazy," said an alarmed Murphy. "I've got powerful people in New York!"

"I'll begin with fingers, though my Comanche friends liked ears," I threatened calmly. I grabbed the woman's arm and flattened her arm on the table top with my knife hovering over her hand. "I could arrest you, Mr. Murphy, but I reckon that's not feasible without a lot of bloodshed."

"Go ahead. She means nothing to me," stated Murphy unfeelingly.

The woman screamed as I cut into her index finger.

"This isn't fair to her, is it?" I let her now bleeding hand go. "I reckon you only care about your own fingers."

Murphy tried but couldn't resist my vice-like grip. A flash of lightning lit up his face but failed to hide the poison in his features.

I flattened his hand on the table top. "Which finger will it be?"

"What do you want, dammit?" pleaded Murphy.

"I reckon there's no point in arresting you." I measured my words. "If you get the hell out of Texas, I'll spare your life. You've seen how I can get to you. You've seen your hired guns fail to get me. You're playing a losing hand, Murphy." I cut his hand to drive home my points. I groped for a threat that would ever reside in the deepest recesses of the man's evil mind. "I won't just kill you. I'll do it the way Comanche killed prisoners, staked out naked with your balls stuffed in your mouth. Do I make myself clear?"

"Damn! I'm bleeding!" he declared. "You cut me, you sonofabitch!"

"You're not hearing me, Mr. Murphy." I began to press on another finger with my knife. "Maybe an ear?" There was an especially bright flash of lightning and a huge clap of thunder, as if to emphasize the message I'd just delivered.

"Okay. Enough." He was sweating profusely. Blood, sweat, and pain have a way of persuading even the evilest of men to obey the victorious hunter.

I threw a towel at him. "I'm leaving. I'll expect to hear that you've taken the first train to New York. Your money is no good here. You'd best never return." I wiped the blood from the knife on a towel. "Sometimes, the Indians cut a man while he's staked and let the ants do their work." I threw that in for effect.

Murphy was already a trembling mess. He shuddered at the image. Lightning lit the room, followed closely by a rolling peal of thunder. It was as though the Devil himself had passed judgment.

I left the man and the whore sitting there half naked and bleeding. The rain had let up, and I could see lightning cast its glow across the horizon, followed by distant thunder. I stopped out into the night.

I didn't spend the night at the hotel but holed up at Union Depot for the night. I'd take the first train out in the morning. Would Gordon Murphy do what I'd told him? I reckoned he was scared enough. Whatever happened when he returned to New York was no concern of mine; at least, not for the present. I'd read about an organization called the Irish Mob and had a suspicion that Murphy was connected with it. Likely as not, I'd headed off the outfit being planted in Texas.

My expectations were met. From my spot in the shadows of the train depot, I watched Murphy with a bandaged hand and three trunks buy his tickets. He never saw me, but I felt pretty good.

TWENTY-ONE
PERDITION CALLS

MY TRAIN RIDE BACK to Corpus Christi was smooth. I was ever cautious. Murphy did seem the vengeful type and might not have called off his dogs. If he was with the Irish Mob, as feared, I had to wonder how far their influence reached. There surely was no honor among thieves or murderers.

I did need to communicate with Captain Hughes. While I hadn't made an arrest, I'd had to use my best judgment. With powerful folks apparently backing him, I figured that Mansfield would likely not have spent a single day in jail, much less found his way to the gallows for engineering so many killings. I reckoned that Hughes would see the wisdom in my actions.

As to Landry Giles, I figured he'd hear of Murphy's departure right quickly, as would Reagan and the Railroad Commission of Texas. The sort of news I'd made tended to travel like greased lightning.

The train screeched, squealed, and belched its way into the Corpus Christi station. I grabbed my satchel and strode up the aisle. Before stepping from the car, I looked up and

down the station platform. It appeared clear but for travelers milling about. It was a beautiful sun-filled day, and I
was confident that I could arrive home before nightfall.
First, I intended to send a telegram to Captain Hughes. It
had been two days since Murphy's departure, but I
doubted word had reached him so far to the south.

The telegrapher was a friendly sort. He waited patiently
while I wrote a cryptic note to my boss.

CAPTAIN JOHN R. HUGHES
    TEXAS RANGERS
    FRONTIER BATTALION, BROWNSVILLE, TX

NEED   PHONE   CALL.   CASE   SOLVED   BUT
COMPLICATED. HOME FOR NEXT DAYS.

LUCAS DUNN, JR
    TEXAS RANGER
    FRONTIER BATTALION

That would have to do it for now. To fully explain by
telegram would break the budget for the Texas Rangers. I
headed off to the stable to fetch the gelding I'd ridden in on.

I slipped the stable boy a bit extra, as I saddled up.

The boy saw my badge and gave me a strange look.
"You the Ranger thet done solved the railroad case?"

How did he know? "Where'd you hear such a thing?"

"Ah kin read. It be in the papers," he informed me.

Somebody had let the news folks know. That my name
was associated was concerning. If I'd been in danger before,

I was in bigger danger now. "Thanks for letting me know." I tipped him a bit more.

"Couple nasty-lookin' men be lookin' fer yuh," he added.

The owner of the stable had watched over my Winchester while I was in Dallas, so I was now very pleased to have it along with the two Smith & Wesson revolvers. I sighed and mounted up. Was I now going to be riding with a target on my back? Had I become the fiery hell in this railroad to perdition?

I rode out of Corpus Christi at a canter. There was no point in delaying the seeming inevitability of being shot at. Where might a bushwhacker be? I held tight to reasonable confidence that my familiarity with the region would serve me well. To that end, I avoided the road from Corpus Christi to Nuecestown and headed much further south.

After a couple of hours of vigilant riding, I stopped for a rest beside a creek with an overhanging pecan tree.

"Wagh!"

I nearly jumped out of my skin.

"Avoidin' them hired guns, eh?" announced Buffalo Watts.

I breathed a bit easier. "Don't be doing that to me."

"Them hired guns be too clumsy tuh git yuh like thet," he observed. "Mind if I foller yuh tuh the ranch?"

I laughed. "Seems you already are, my friend."

"Yuh e'er seen one of these afore?" Watts thrust a green leafy thing at me.

"That's a shamrock. Where'd you find it?"

Watts shrugged. "It were pinned to yer barn door."

Thoughts of Murphy and the Irish MOB shot through

my brain. Seemed that Nuecestown wasn't out of reach. "Let's ride, Buffalo."

We decided not to approach Heaven's Gate Ranch through the archway, but to come in from the south. We split up.

Clumsy was an understatement as concerned Murphy's hired guns. There were three of them hidden in an arroyo that ran along the lane from the gateway arch to the big house. I wondered whether they realized that they weren't on a payroll anymore? No matter for the present. I motioned to Watts to circle around. We'd get the bush-whackers in a sort of crossfire from behind them.

I stalked to within about twenty feet of the three. The first thing they heard was me levering a round into the chamber of my Winchester. "Y'all can drop those guns and raise your hands. You're under arrest."

Taken fully by surprise, they turned in unison with mouths gaping. The tallest of the trio pointed his carbine in my direction, but my finger was far faster than his. A hole appeared where his nose had been. He was a dead man standing.

The other two were considering their options when they heard Watts off to their left as he chambered a round. They dropped their rifles.

"Keep them in your sights, Buffalo," I said as I strode forward with manacles. As I began to cuff the two of them together, I heard a voice from the direction of the big house.

"Let 'em go, Dunn, you sonofabitch, or I'll kill your family."

Watts and I froze. That cowardly, lily-livered skunk Kyle McClintock was holding my family hostage.

I clobbered both gunmen up the side of their heads. When they came to, they might leave, but they would be manacled together.

"The man who was paying you is gone, McClintock. It's over. Let my family go." I tentatively walked toward the house. I could see Cassie tied to a gallery support with Sean and Bode seated beside her, crying with fear. McClintock stood with Cassie between us.

"Drop your gun, Junior. This ain't about railroads."

This was personal. McClintock had never forgiven me for winning Cassie's favor. There was no standoff at play here. Either McClintock or I was going to die. I laid my Winchester on the ground.

Cassie looked fearless, but I knew she was scared.

McClintock smiled at me, as he ran his hand up Cassie's body and grabbed a breast. "Come on, Junior." He motioned me to head toward him.

EPILOGUE

THE NUECES STRIP of 1897 was still mostly a vast prairie of tall grasses and loamy-sands stretching far as the eye could see and beyond. Grasses tended to grow high enough to reach a horse's withers, though stands of live oak, mesquite, and prickly pear cactus brought to the prairie from the south, mostly by seed-carrying birds and by cattle droppings, had already begun to proliferate. Winds blowing through the wiregrass created their own special music. Brush proliferated, often creating nearly impenetrable barriers owing to the density and occasional thorniness.

The Nueces Strip, called Wild Horse Desert by some, reached south from the lazily flowing Nueces River all the way to the meandering Rio Grande along Texas' southern border. Its eastern extremity enjoyed the sea breezes wafting in off the Gulf of Mexico from Corpus Christi all the way to Brownsville. Nestled in hills at its northern extreme was the little town of Uvalde, while the semi-arid rolling terrain of Laredo was generally regarded as its far western reach. Rough but serviceable roads were being carved out of the Strip and mostly paralleled the railroads, which had begun to proliferate. Texas enjoyed a veritable steel spiderweb of interconnecting railroads. A form of creative destruction was in full flower.

Despite its uninviting landscape, South Texas drew all sorts of opportunists like moths to a light bulb. Texas still remained a prime destination for second chancers, folks who'd met with rough times and looked to restart their lives. Towns, farms, and ranches sprang up at a record pace. They were pressed to conquer a challenging terrain.

Much of Texas history centers around the Nueces Strip. No discussion of it can ever be complete without mention that much of the most significant fighting of the Texas War for Independence was fought on and just north of the Nueces Strip back in 1835 and 1836. It was also the scene of the first skirmishes of the Mexican-American War of 1846. The Strip was officially ceded to the United States by the Treaty of Guadalupe Hidalgo in 1848, though Texas had already laid claim.

The plentiful and accessible longhorn were for years the low-hanging-fruit of the Nueces Strip economy. They were a hardy breed that could withstand the South Texas heat, fend off disease-carrying pests, and carry just enough meat on their bones to make them reasonably profitable to raise. Originally brought from the Iberian Peninsula by early Spanish priests, the longhorns eventually escaped the mostly failing missionaries, proliferated, and roamed wild and free across the prairies.

Millions of the beasts soon covered Texas and especially the excellent grazing lands of the Nueces Strip. They competed with those wild mustangs that had also been introduced by the Spaniards. Ranchers were increasingly importing and breeding meatier, shorter-horned breeds like Brahmans, Angus, Herefords, and even Richard King's

Santa Gertrudis. Of course, there had been the indigenous buffalo, millions of the beasts. They'd been a staple of the Comanche peoples' way of life until their hides were taken in wholesale slaughters to enrich eastern merchants and scions of fashion. The Texas prairies nevertheless provided plenty of feed for all.

The factor that would ultimately win the west was the family; the larger the better, as children grew up in the face of all manner of lurking dangers. Families established the ranches and farms popping up not only throughout the eastern portions of the Nueces Strip but across Texas as a whole. People sought fresh opportunities. The territory east of the 98th meridian sliced through the very heart of Texas, which was fast becoming an economic juggernaut, and the Strip was no exception. Its economy was based on growing cotton and raising cattle and horses. Cotton was bundled and hauled to port for transport to markets in Louisiana and points east, while cattle were driven mostly to Texas slaughterhouses. Indians were pushed ever westward, as tribes were overcome by a cocktail of socioeconomic forces, violent conflict, and disease.

While the frontier grew ever westward, there remained ongoing worry about the threats posed by rogue off-reservation Comanche, Kiowa, and Lipan Apache, as well as the marauding bandits from south of the Rio Grande and lawbreaking opportunists from the east. This all served to keep early Texans on this wild and often lawless frontier ever vigilant. It was easy to make the case for calling up companies of Texas Rangers to patrol the Nueces Strip, as they took it upon themselves to go where the military found it politically undesirable. On the other hand, the legislators in the state capital in Austin often were unable to pull together the financial means to fund the necessary companies of Rangers. They had to rely on the US Army, which could be chancy at best, as it was subject to the politics of whoever was in power and the perceiving of real or imagined threats.

Thus, the setting for the Tumbleweed Sagas: Junior's Story series is hardly any less challenging than mere decades before. Yet civilization marches inexorably onward, taming the remaining frontier.

A LOOK AT

NICHOLAS DUNN: THE MAKING OF A TEXAS LEGEND

From Irish roots to a Texas legend.

In 1850, fifteen-year-old Nicholas Dunn lands in Corpus Christi, Texas, fleeing famine-stricken Ireland with nothing but grit, red hair, and two uncles by his side. What follows is an epic, true-life saga that spans six decades across the untamed South Texas plains.

Fiercely loyal to his family and Catholic faith, Nicholas becomes a master horseman, a shrewd livestock trader, and a man both feared and admired. Through love, loss, and bloodshed, he builds a legacy on the rugged Nueces Strip—raising a family and earning a reputation as a bold, unbreakable Texan.

Nicholas Dunn: The Making of a Texas Legend is a sweeping first-person biography of an Irish immigrant who carved his name into the very soil of the American West. From blacksmithing and failed crops to cattle drives, Indian skirmishes, and standoffs with Mexican bandits, Dunn's journey is marked by peril, persistence, and a relentless pursuit of purpose.

Blending Irish fire with cowboy grit, Dunn's story echoes the spirit of the Old West while offering a deeply personal glimpse into the making of a legend.

AVAILABLE NOW

ACKNOWLEDGMENTS

Authoring books simply doesn't happen in a vacuum. While the author provides the creative talent and crafts the stories, there is much more that demands acknowledgment. There are many folks and places that contribute to my authoring endeavors. So, it is with *Railroad to Perdition: Justice Rides an Iron Horse*. It takes place in 1897. The newly wrought exploits of the son of legendary Texas Ranger Captain Luke Dunn were at the core of the Sagas, but the Junior's Story series stands apart. Lucas Dunn Junior symbolizes the lawman image, the pursuer of law and order in the person of a hero, protector, knight-errant sort of character. But there's much more to him. He carries on a family legacy of grit, tenacity, rugged individualism, and bravery, nuanced with a masculine vulnerability and a search for redeeming values. He epitomizes the freedom of America's western frontier and represents a final bastion of honor in America. Hopefully, readers will find *Railroad to Perdition: Justice Rides an Iron Horse* an adventure worthy of their time and emotional involvement.

I've been blessed with many friends and family who have supported my writings. My wife Carolyn's reviews and encouragement were a huge help, along with very important tech support from our sons Mike and Matt. Other supporters have included Cara Miller, Jim May, Ernie Angell, Chris Haug, and my dear cousins Johnny Dunn, Jim & Cindy Holmgreen, Francette Meaney, and Eddie and

Nancy Thornton. Many more friends have contributed support at some level to the creation and publication of my books, including this *Railroad to Perdition: Justice Rides an Iron Horse,* be it encouragement or advice.

Naturally, I am majorly grateful to the great folks at Wolfpack Publishing. The team they bring to publishing is first rate, from editing to typesetting to cover design and the myriad tasks that lead to successful book sales.

It's only right to acknowledge my ancestors who were actual settlers of the South Texas frontier. In addition to inspiring me, they provided a quite helpful true-to-life framework as to the life and times on the Texas Nueces Strip. It was appropriate to weave them into the tapestry of my western novels. Matthew Dunn (1809-1863) immigrated to Corpus Christi from County Kildare in 1845, established a homestead on Upriver Road in Nuecestown, and served as a sutler to General Zachary Taylor's Army in the Mexican-American War. Peter Dunn (1807-1890) immigrated from Ireland in 1850 and established a black-smith shop in Corpus Christi; John Dunn (1803-1889) ranched and grew thousands of acres of cotton; Lawrence Dunn (1837-1864) fought and died with Captain Ware's Confederate cavalry; and my great-great-grandfather Nicholas Dunn (1835-1912) was a rancher, drover, livestock speculator, marksman, and Comanche fighter of some repute. My cousin John Beamond *Red John* Dunn (1851-1940) served as a Texas Ranger in the 1870s under Captain Bland Chamberlain (Company H), subsequently joined a vigilance committee, became a farmer and merchant, and curated a museum of military weapons displayed to this day in the Corpus Christi Museum of Science & History. Red John Dunn's brother Matthew Dunn also served as a Texas Ranger, and another cousin, Rut Evans, served as a Texas Ranger in the 1890s (Company E, Frontier Battalion,

Alice, TX). My cousin Patrick Dunn was quite successful at raising longhorns on North Padre Island east of Corpus Christi from 1883 to 1937. John Hillard Dunn (1883-1958), whose personal narrative about his family and his own adventures drove my pursuit of my Texas family, inspired my own writings, and led me to write his yet-to-be-published biography, *Tough Hombre—Recollections of a True Texan*. Finally, my grandfather, Horace Charles Greathouse, served as a Texas Ranger in 1920 (Company C, Austin, TX). Such real-life characters, coupled with actual events, have served to reinforce the historical settings for my writings.

Most of my authoring has occurred in my office as decorated to channel my inner Texan, but my creative juices have often been inspired and imagination stoked in cafés and coffee houses across America. My favorites were Hester's Café & Coffee Bar in Corpus Christi, TX; Nueces Café in Robstown, TX; Java Ranch Espresso Bar & Café in Fredericksburg, TX; PAX Coffee & Goods in Kerrville, TX; Ragged Edge Coffee House and Bantam Coffee Roasters in Gettysburg, PA; 1889 Coffee House in Helena, MT; Dunn Brothers Coffee in Rapid City, SD; Postmasters Coffee & Bakery and Brio Coffeehouse in Waynesboro, PA; Birdie's Café and American Ice Co Café in Westminster, MD; and Baltimore Coffee & Tea Co., Frederick Coffee Company & Café, and Dublin Roasters in Frederick, MD; Deja Brew Coffee in New Oxford, PA; and Deja Brew at Miney Branch in Carroll Valley, PA. And yes, I've quaffed my share of coffee at Dunkin' Donuts and Starbucks around America. The décors and easy listening music in these fine establishments, combined with friendly clientele and savory cups of coffee, tended to set me in the right creative frame of mind. They also afforded engagement with many fine citizens of our nation.

Last but not least, I'm especially thankful for the many folks who have read and enjoyed my books.

I do believe it is important to acknowledge how the old west represents the brave pioneering spirit of settlers who met the challenges and transcended mere survival to enable America to achieve exceptional growth. The settling of the American west is replete with tales of leveraging freedom for individual achievement. I hope you will agree that reliving our past—even through history-based fiction—often has the effect of pointing the way to an ever-brighter future. Might we be up to it? I hope that the inspiration I have drawn from my having walked the very earth my characters have trodden, coupled with my extensive historical research, will enable readers to fully experience the grit, adventure, and passion of my characters while sensing aromas of gunsmoke, trail dust, leather, sweat, and bluebonnets.

Thanks kindly to all of you.

ABOUT THE AUTHOR

 Multiple-award-winning author Mark Greathouse is a fifth-generation Texan devoted to history and writing western genre fiction. He has published fourteen western novels, an anthology, and a biography, as well as published western history articles in various magazines and newspapers. He received a 2025 Western Writers of America Spur Finalist Award for Short Fiction with "Prairie Dog" published in a local anthology. *Guns on the Guadalupe: Justice on the River,* published by Wolfpack Publishing, continues Greathouse's passion for weaving fiction in a historical setting. He crafts an engaging adventure, featuring an ensemble of captivating characters woven into compellingly complex subplots. Importantly, he has stayed true to the western story being America's morality story, as good triumphs over evil. Whether expressed in his epic western genre novels or adventure-laced biographies, he couples a soul-penetrating creative spirit with extensive historical research that attracts a broad spectrum of readers. Greathouse is a member of Western Writers of America and several poetry societies. He holds BA and MBA degrees. Greathouse lives in Southern Pennsylvania but travels west regularly to walk in the footsteps of his characters.

www.ingramcontent.com/pod-product-compliance
Lightning Source LLC
Chambersburg PA
CBHW011517240626
47154CB00010B/3061